IT HAPPENED ONE PLIGHT

BOBBI SUE BAXTER MYSTERIES BOOK 4

Marissa Shrock

It Happened One Plight

Published by Cimelia Press, Greentown, Indiana

Printed in the United States of America

Print ISBN-13: 979-8-9921305-1-5

Library of Congress Control Number: 2026902403

AUTHOR'S NOTE

Just as Wildcat Springs, Indiana, is a figment of my imagination, so are many of the other towns and locations I created in this story.

CHAPTER 1

JULY 1988

I SHOULD'VE KNOWN my first official date with Hemi Miller would be anything but normal. My summer at home in Wildcat Springs, Indiana, continued to offer twists and turns, and our picnic in Sycamore Park on a sunny Wednesday evening proved to be no exception.

The public pool had closed, and screaming kids had gone home, leaving the park peaceful as a gentle breeze rustled the leaves of the towering sycamore tree. A hyper yellow Labrador retriever dragged a frazzled middle-aged woman toward the trail while two teenage boys tossed a frisbee. A jogger wearing a Walkman breezed past us.

Hemi plopped a basket on a picnic table under a small pavilion. "Well, Bobbi Sue, I'm not much of a cook, so this isn't fancy." His intelligent brown eyes sparkled. "But I made chocolate chip cookies—from scratch. It's my mother's recipe." He took a container of sandwiches from the basket.

I pushed my sunglasses onto my head and hoped her baking was better than her prickly personality. "I love cookies." We didn't need to get into my issues with his mother Amanda—or his own problems with her, for that matter.

"Cool."

I smothered a sigh. In the time it'd taken us to walk across the street from Hemi's house to the park, we'd covered the weather, my sister Rochelle's pregnancy, and now we were discussing dessert. I could just imagine the headline: "Cookies Provide Conversational Lifeline for Adults Battling Junior-High Awkwardness."

Maybe I'd misinterpreted his invitation. Maybe this wasn't a date, and we were hanging out as friends. Was I making him uncomfortable because he sensed *I* thought it was a date, but that wasn't his intention? Were my sundress and painted fingernails overkill? Should I have chosen denim shorts and a T-shirt? But he'd acted nervous yesterday when he'd stopped by while I was working my shift waiting tables at Chuckie's Chicken. He'd rambled a few minutes before finally asking me to join him on a picnic.

My friend Misty Ambrose hadn't doubted the picnic was a date. "What else would it be?" she'd asked earlier today when she'd come to help me decide what to wear.

"He's bored and still getting over his fiancée?"

Misty popped a hand on her hip. "The one he dumped for you?"

"That's not quite what happened." Hemi and Leslie hadn't been right for each other, but she *was* pretty. Did he regret letting her go?

I was slender and fairly attractive with brown, shoulder-length hair and blue eyes. But what if I wasn't enough for a guy who shared a strong resemblance to Matt Dillon?

"Keep telling yourself that," Misty had said as she'd scrutinized my closet.

Shaking off my insecurities, I reached into the picnic basket and removed a plastic baggie of carrots. Across the park, one of the frisbee boys leaped to catch the disc but missed and plunked onto his backside.

"Bobbi Sue?"

"Yeah?" I pulled my attention back to Hemi, who was looking cute in a blue button-down shirt and khaki shorts.

"I asked if you'd heard from your parents since the letter?"

"Sorry. No, I haven't." I sat at the paint-chipped table as relief flooded over me because we finally had something natural to discuss. "But I have news."

He took a Coke from the basket, popped off the cap, and handed over the bottle. "Sounds ominous." He sat across from me, concern flooding his brown eyes.

"It might be." I sipped the Coke. "The other day, FBI Special Agent Cole Erickson stopped in the restaurant while I was working. He had questions for my dad and wondered if I knew where he and Mom were."

"What'd you tell him?"

"As little as possible, but I learned we've most likely been wrong about why my parents disappeared last month."

Hemi furrowed his brow. "How so?"

"All this time, Grandma, my sister, and I thought they fled because Dad was afraid of the publicity surrounding the Ross Garland murder case."

"You thought it might tip off the drug lord who'd vowed revenge after your dad was exonerated and released from prison."

"Exactly," I said. "But Victor Delacruz died in May, and his family couldn't care less about my dad. The craziest part is that Special Agent Erickson already told my dad that Delacruz was dead."

Hemi furrowed his brow. "Why didn't your dad tell you and your sister?"

"I have no idea."

"Did Special Agent Erickson say anything else?"

"He wanted to know if I'd heard from my parents."

"Did you tell him about their letter?" Hemi asked.

My mom had written us a letter to assure us they were safe, and someone had left it in my grandma's mail slot.

"No."

He shifted. "Then what'd you say?"

"I said I hadn't heard from them—because I haven't heard their voices."

"You lied to a federal agent?" He looked around, but unless the squirrels scampering up the trees were government spies, we were safe from eavesdroppers.

"I didn't lie," I said. "I haven't *heard* from them."

"I doubt your reasoning would hold up in court." He opened the container, put a ham and cheese sandwich onto a paper plate, and handed it to me.

"I didn't feel like being transparent with a total stranger, even if he has a badge and a gun." I also didn't have blind trust in law enforcement—not after what'd happened to my dad.

"I don't understand why Special Agent Erickson needs to see your dad."

"He wants to talk to him about Morris Fulton, who did time with my dad. When I asked why, Special Agent Erickson wouldn't tell me. He dodged my question about Dad being in danger. He just tossed me a business card and told me to reach out if I heard from them."

Hemi took a sandwich for himself. "So your new theory is that your parents fled because of something to do with Morris Fulton."

"Who was recently released from prison."

"What do you know about Fulton?" Hemi studied me.

"Not much, so I called Juanita St. James and left a message about the FBI agent's visit. I'd like to see what *she* knows about Fulton."

Juanita was my mom's college roommate and the investigative reporter who'd helped find the truth that'd cleared my father's name years earlier when he'd been convicted for a murder he hadn't committed. She was my inspiration and why I was studying journalism at the University of Northern Indiana. Her motto, "the truth always matters," drove me to dig for answers and had helped me solve a few murder cases this summer.

"What's your grandma think?" Hemi opened a potato chip bag.

"I haven't told her."

"When she finds out you kept this from her, it won't be pretty."

"I was hoping to find answers from Juanita first."

"Since the FBI agent talked to you at work, your grandma's probably heard." He held out the chips.

I grabbed a handful and dropped them onto my plate. "It's only been a couple of days, and the restaurant was practically empty." I bit into my sandwich, but doubt tightened my stomach. Gossip spread quickly in our small town.

"When we're done eating, we should walk to your grandma's house, so you can come clean."

I nearly choked. No guy in his right mind would suggest a detour to Grandma's house if this were a date. If Hemi didn't already know Grandma, I'd hide him until we were an official couple, lest she scare him away with questions about the number of children he wanted to sire.

She'd done it before.

I swallowed. "I'll call her tomorrow."

Hemi took a carrot stick from the bag. "If you say so."

"It's time I tried one of those cookies." *Back to the trusty dessert topic.*

He handed me the container, and as I took one, my gaze landed on a woman striding toward us with a messenger bag slung across her chest. She wore sunglasses and had dark blond hair cut in feathery layers, and her black pantsuit accentuated her tall and commanding frame. Dropping my cookie onto a napkin, I squinted. Surely it couldn't be.

Hemi followed my gaze. "You know her?"

I stood as she came closer. "That's Juanita St. James."

CHAPTER 2

"YOU'RE A TOUGH GIRL TO FIND." Juanita ripped off her sunglasses and hooked them in her camisole as she approached Hemi and me. "I drove out to your house in those creepy woods. Don't know why your folks built that beautiful stone house in the boonies where no one can see it. When you weren't home, I went to Chuckie's Chicken. By the way, why are you selling yourself short working there, honey? I could've gotten you an internship at a paper somewhere. Anywhere. I have so many connections. Did you even think to ask for my help?" She put her hands on her hips.

My face grew warm. "I should've."

"Anyway, your tubby boss told me you might be at Tate's Place since you hang out there. So, I schlepped over. The bartender was mum, but the redhead flirting with him said she's a friend of yours and spilled the beans that you were on a date with Hemingway Miller in Sycamore Park. I assume that's you." She pointed at Hemi but didn't wait for a response and thrust out her hand. "Juanita St. James."

He stood and grasped her hand. "Hemi Miller."

"Nice to meet you," she said. "Not surprised to hear you

don't go by Hemingway. That's a mouthful for a first name. Classy though. I'm a fan of Ernest's writing."

"So were my parents." Hemi appeared shellshocked, and I couldn't blame him. "But I've always been grateful they picked *Hemingway* instead of *Ernest*."

"As you should be." She turned to me. "I'm sorry to interrupt your date, but we need to chat."

I wished she'd stop referencing our date. But I said, "I appreciate you coming."

She opened her arms. "Give me a hug. It's been ages."

I walked around the table, and as she embraced me, she said to Hemi, "She's like the daughter I never had." She let go and stepped back. "How long have you two been dating?"

"Uh—not long." Hemi glanced at me.

Either he didn't mind this ambush as much as I feared, or he was just being polite.

"Well, then, Bobbi Sue. I'll leave it up to you if you want to include this young man in our discussion. My gut says he's a good one, and I'm rarely wrong, but it's your call."

I may not have been sure about this outing's status, but I *was* certain about trusting Hemi. "You can talk in front of him. He's got my back."

He met my gaze, and from the gleam in his eyes, I could tell my response pleased him.

"All right." She pointed at the table, and we sat.

"Would you like anything to eat?" Hemi asked. "I brought plenty." He held out the sandwich container.

"Don't mind if I do. I'm starving because I forgot to eat lunch." She grabbed a sandwich and took a bite. After she swallowed, she said, "I was working on a huge story, so I'm sorry I haven't had time to dig into why your parents disappeared. How have you been coping with that plot twist?"

"I'm hanging in there. A few weeks ago, Grandma found a

letter in her mailbox from Mom and Dad assuring us they're safe, but they didn't tell us where they are."

"Where was the letter postmarked?" She took another bite.

"It wasn't," I said. "Someone hand delivered it, and we thought maybe it was you."

"I haven't been to Indiana in ages." Juanita grabbed a handful of chips.

"Do you know who they would've trusted to deliver the letter if they didn't do it themselves?" Hemi asked.

She popped a chip into her mouth and appeared to consider the options. "No. But that doesn't mean anything. I haven't kept in touch with Guy and Nicki like I should've."

"What brings you to Wildcat Springs?" Hemi asked. "Is Bobbi Sue in danger?"

Juanita studied him with her intense gaze. "How would you feel if I answered *yes*?"

"Well . . . I . . ." He shifted. "I'd do everything I could to protect her."

"Hemi knows Krav Maga," I said.

His cheeks turned pink. Why'd I felt the need to blurt that out?

"What's that?" Juanita asked.

"A fighting system developed by the Israeli Defense Forces," Hemi said. "I can use it for self-defense—if necessary."

"Good for you." She glanced back and forth between us as if she couldn't quite figure us out.

We needed a topic change—fast. "Are you here because of what you found on Morris Fulton?"

"Yes, but before I get into that, there's something else you need to know." Juanita set her sandwich on the plate and brushed crumbs from her hands. "I don't think your parents ever wanted you and Rochelle to find out, but we're at the point where we don't have a choice."

I braced myself. "Okay . . ."

"Prison changed your dad, even though he wasn't guilty," she said. "He doesn't trust the system, and who can blame him? He told me that he wondered if a wrongful conviction happened to him, how many other people had the system failed? So, he vowed to fight for people the way I fought for him."

"Is Morris Fulton one of them?" I asked.

"Yes. After serving time with Fulton and hearing his story, Guy thought the evidence in Fulton's case was weak, and the more your dad got to know him, the more certain he became that Fulton wouldn't have killed his girlfriend."

"So after Dad was freed, he took it upon himself to investigate?"

"You got it," she said. "Years ago, after your family moved to Wildcat Springs, your dad asked me to send everything I could find on Morris Fulton's case, and I did."

"Mom approved of the investigation?"

"She understood—even though she wasn't thrilled. Your dad may have investigated other cases, but he's never asked me for information on anyone but Fulton. It took years for your dad to find the truth about what really happened in Fulton's case."

All this time, Dad had been playing detective. He certainly had a lot of secrets that I'd learned about this summer. "You didn't think to clue me in that Dad's little side project could be the reason he and Mom disappeared?"

"Like I said, it'd been years since I'd helped. Until you called and told me that FBI agent asked about Fulton, I didn't make the connection."

Hemi glanced at her with a hint of suspicion in his eyes. "What can you tell us about Fulton?"

"He's thirty-eight and from Wabash Ridge, Illinois. He was convicted of killing his ex-girlfriend Sandra McDonald," Juanita said. "A busybody neighbor testified to hearing Fulton and

McDonald argue, and police found a knife with McDonald's blood type in the dumpster at Fulton's complex. Fulton swore he wasn't at his girlfriend's apartment that night, but he didn't have an alibi."

"There weren't any other suspects?" I asked.

"Not at the time." Juanita shook her head. "Long story short, your dad discovered McDonald's other neighbor moved to Missouri the day after the murder and before someone found McDonald's body, so no one interviewed her. Until your dad found her, she didn't know about Fulton's conviction. She heard Sandra McDonald arguing with her sister that night. Then, your dad figured out the busybody neighbor had been diagnosed with dementia shortly after testifying. Eventually, McDonald's sister confessed to stabbing her and putting the knife in the dumpster to frame Fulton." She opened her messenger bag, withdrew a manila folder, and dropped it onto the table. "The article on top talks about why Fulton was released in March of this year—and gives a case overview."

I set the newspaper article on the table for Hemi to read. I skimmed it, but Juanita had summarized Fulton's case well. "This doesn't help us figure out why Fulton was looking for my dad or why Special Agent Erickson cares."

"Exactly." Juanita nodded. "Fulton moved home to Wabash Ridge after being released, so I stopped there on my way here this morning. He's been working at a grocery store. The manager told me Fulton quit a couple of days ago, and he had no clue why. Said Fulton had been living with his sister, Lucia, so I tracked her down. She confirmed her brother quit his job and packed for a road trip to see a buddy in Pennsylvania. He left yesterday afternoon. Care to guess where he planned to stop on the way?"

"In Wildcat Springs to see my dad?"

"You got it."

CHAPTER 3

"DOES Fulton have business with Dad? Or is he hoping to thank Dad in person?" I asked Juanita as I glanced around the park to make sure no one was within earshot. Thankfully, nobody seemed to notice us.

"Fulton's sister Lucia said he'd promised to help your dad with other cases if his conviction was overturned and had been communicating with Guy about that possibility. She figured that's why her brother was on the FBI's radar, but none of us know for sure." Juanita put the last bite of her ham sandwich into her mouth.

"Is there anything else you learned from Fulton's sister?" Hemi asked.

Juanita swallowed. "Guy promised to send a file about a potential case, and when he didn't, Fulton got worried—especially when he didn't hear anything else."

I furrowed my brow. "I wonder if it was a dangerous case, and Fulton wanted to check on Dad."

"I'd say they all have the potential to be dangerous." Juanita said. "And the new case could be what prompted your parents to leave."

Hemi looked at me. "Have any strangers called the house looking for your dad?"

"No. Fulton might've contacted Dad's construction company office instead. I'll check with his business manager." I'd been stacking my parents' mail in Dad's office, and if there'd been a letter from Fulton, I hadn't noticed. "Did Lucia say when the communication stopped?"

"A few weeks ago," Juanita said.

"Right around the time Mom and Dad left." My mind whirled as I tried to make sense of the new information. "I wonder if Fulton came to the house while I was at work yesterday or today." I studied his picture with the article. He was thin, with sad eyes and a prominent nose. "I haven't seen him out and about."

Hemi looked over my shoulder. "I haven't either."

"He might still be in the area, so we should try to find him," Juanita said.

"I agree." I turned to Hemi. "What do you think?"

"I'm in," he said.

I glanced at Juanita before turning my attention back to Hemi. "I'm sorry this evening isn't turning out like we'd planned."

"No problem." He clasped my hand. "Getting answers about your parents is more important than a picnic. We can always try again."

My heart fluttered at the warmth in his voice—and gaze.

"All right. Here's the game plan." Juanita clapped her hands and shattered our trance. "I'll check the cheap motels in Richardville since Fulton probably has a tight budget. You two ask around Wildcat Springs to see if he's appeared at any local joints. If we find him, we'll ask what he knows about the feds, what Guy was working on, and why Guy and Nicki might've left. We'll meet back at your parents' house when we're done."

"You're staying with me, right?" I asked. "Mom always keeps the guest room ready." I wasn't going to make any promises about serving a great breakfast, but Juanita would have a comfortable bed.

"That sounds great. Thanks. I'd rather not drive back to Chicago tonight." She glanced at her watch. "Let's roll." She untangled her long legs from underneath the picnic bench and strode toward the parking lot.

Shaking my head, I dropped the carrot bag into Hemi's picnic basket. "I'm having trouble processing what just happened. Mom always called her Hurricane Juanita, and now I completely understand."

"Perfect nickname." He watched her zoom out of the parking lot as he placed the sandwich container in the basket. "Want to try Tate's Place first?"

"Yeah." I was thankful Hemi was such a good sport. "Let's just hope someone's seen Fulton."

"Nope." Kurt Conway, the bartender and manager at Tate's Place, looked at Morris Fulton's picture as "Higher Love" played on the juke box. "That guy hasn't been in here." He studied me with his icy blue eyes. "What's going on, Bobbi Snoop? Why're you looking for a criminal?"

Hemi furrowed his brow. "His conviction was overturned, so he's not a criminal. He came to see Bobbi Sue's dad, and we want to know why." He glanced at me as if waiting to see if I'd add anything, but I didn't feel the need.

"Hmph." Kurt looked back and forth between us. "You asked Misty if this guy's staying at the inn?"

"I will," I said. "But a room at the inn might be out of Fulton's budget, so we didn't start there. Is she working tonight?" Misty's mom owned and operated Creekside Inn, which wasn't far from my house in Wildcat Woods. Misty helped there when she wasn't working as a nanny.

"Yep. She left here about an hour ago." There was no mistaking the disappointment in Kurt's expression.

He really just needed to ask Misty out on a date. "Thanks for your—"

"I mighta seen him," a man said.

We directed our attention to a pudgy, middle-aged guy in a gray suit sitting a few stools away from where we stood. I'd seen him here before, and he'd been a customer at Chuckie's Chicken. He put his half empty beer mug on the counter and wiggled his fingers. "Lemme see that picture you got."

I walked over to the man, held out the clipping, and pointed to the picture. "Is this the man?"

He studied it. "Yes siree Bob. Earlier today, I was in line paying for gas over at the service station on the east end of town, and this man was ahead of me asking the clerk for directions to Guy Baxter's office. Seemed important." The man surveyed me with admiration in his beady-eyed gaze. "You're Guy's daughter, right?"

Hemi moved closer and rested a hand on my shoulder.

I tried to appear pleasant instead of creeped out by this man's knowledge of me. "Yes, I'm Bobbi Sue."

He waved a hand. "Oh, I know. Your dad did a renovation for me a few years back, and I've seen ya in here and at the chicken place. You're the girl who saw the alien in the woods. Am I right?"

I was never, ever going to live that down. "That's not quite what—"

"I don't believe I caught your name, sir." Hemi reached around me and extended his hand.

"My apologies." He stuck out a chubby paw and shook Hemi's hand with gusto. "Stan Stanton."

Oh wow. What'd his parents been thinking? "What gave you the impression that it was important for Fulton to find my dad's office?"

"He was stressed and upset," Stan said.

"Upset with Mr. Baxter?" Hemi rested his hand on the small of my back.

"I couldn't tell, but he looked desperate to find him. Seems he might've mentioned that he had something important for Guy. The kid working the register had no idea where the office was, so I stepped in and saved the day."

Funny how he wanted to portray himself as a hero. "What time was that?" I asked.

He glanced at his Rolex. "Around four-thirty. I remember thinking he'd better hurry because the office probably closes at five like other businesses."

"It does," I said. "Do you remember anything else?"

He shifted and took a swig of beer. "I hate to speculate and get somebody in trouble."

"A little conjecture never hurt." I leaned against the bar. "No one's necessarily in trouble."

"All right," Stan said. "His pant leg was caught on his ankle sheath, and I could see a knife."

Goosebumps rose on my arms, and I was glad that I'd put on my jean jacket over my sundress. Had Dad misjudged Fulton? Just because he was innocent of killing his girlfriend didn't mean he wasn't dangerous. "Thanks, Mr. Stanton. You've been helpful." I turned back to Kurt. "Do you mind if we use your office phone?" I braced myself for an argument and an order to use the pay phone.

Instead, with concern in his expression, Kurt glanced at Stan. "Go ahead—as long as it's local."

"It is—and thanks." I led Hemi to Kurt's office and closed the door. "I need to call my dad's business manager to see if she saw Fulton—and to make sure she's all right."

"Fulton may've been armed to protect himself." Hemi handed me the phonebook.

"But we don't know for sure."

"Just considering all the possibilities."

With trembling fingers, I thumbed through the pages until I found Eileen Donahue's home number and dialed. As the phone rang, my heart rate increased.

"Hello." Eileen sounded weary.

"Eileen, it's Bobbi Sue."

"I don't suppose you're calling to tell me your dad's coming home. I'm getting so tired of saying I don't know what's going on or when he'll be back to take care of people's problems."

"I'm sorry. I'm hoping they'll be home before school starts next month." My mom was an elementary teacher who loved her job, so I couldn't imagine her staying away.

But I never would've guessed they'd leave in the first place.

"I figured, but you never know." Eileen heaved a sigh. "What's going on?"

I twisted the phone cord around my wrist. "When you were at work today, did you get a visit from a guy named Morris Fulton?"

Hemi stepped closer to listen, and I tipped the receiver so he could hear.

"No, but I closed early because my youngest kid was puking, and I had to pick him up from the babysitter."

"What time did you leave?"

"Around three-thirty or so."

"Did Bruce come to the office today?" Bruce Reynolds was my dad's foreman.

"He was working on-site with the crew at the Keller house,

so unless he stopped by after I left, he wasn't around either," she said. "Is something wrong?"

"Not necessarily. I heard Fulton was looking for my dad, and I'd like to know why." Eileen didn't need to know about Special Agent Erickson's questions.

"I have no clue." A child's wail sounded over the line, and she groaned. "Sorry. Gotta go deal with more vomit. Oh, the joys of motherhood." She hung up.

I faced Hemi who hovered close to me. "Let's swing by my dad's office."

He checked his watch. "If Fulton went there right after he talked to Stan, he's long gone."

"I know," I said. "But Stan thought Fulton had something for my dad, so maybe he left it when he realized no one was there."

"All right." He grasped my hand and led me out of the bar to his Bronco parked outside. "I meant to tell you earlier that you look beautiful in that dress." He opened the passenger door for me.

My face warmed. "Thank you."

In the midst of this chaotic evening, I was now sure about one thing.

Our picnic really had been a date.

Dad's construction company office and warehouse were located on Walnut Street near the edge of town. After he'd been released from prison, we'd moved to Wildcat Springs, my mom's hometown, for a fresh start. He'd opened Baxter Construction, and we'd lived quietly for over ten years until this past June.

Hemi drove around the warehouse where Dad stored materials and equipment, and when we didn't see anything unusual, he parked next to the office building. "Do you have a key?"

I held up my keys. "Dad left these behind, so I put them on my ring in case I needed them."

We got out of the Bronco and walked to the back door. Stillness blanketed the street, interrupted only by the office's rumbling air conditioner. I checked the stoop and peeked behind a hydrangea bush.

"Nothing." Though I wasn't surprised, I was a little disappointed.

"Let's look out front," Hemi said.

I unlocked the back door, and Hemi brushed past me and turned on the lights. I entered and locked the door behind us.

When we rounded a corner, Hemi froze. "Why's *that* light on?" The fluorescent lights hummed as he pointed to a beam from my dad's office illuminating the hallway.

"Eileen probably forgot it because she left in a hurry." But with Dad out of town, why would she have been in his office at all?

With Hemi on my heels, I passed the conference room and Eileen's spotless desk in the reception area decorated with photos of houses that Dad's company had built. When I looked into Dad's office, I screamed, and my hand flew to my mouth.

Next to an open filing cabinet, a man lay prone in a pool of blood.

CHAPTER 4

HEMI LUNGED FORWARD, knelt next to the man, and checked his pulse. "He's gone."

Trying not to look at the gunshot wound on the man's back, I studied the side of his face, and his prominent nose. "It's Morris Fulton."

Hemi stood and rested a hand on my back. "I know."

I closed my eyes as the situation's injustice rolled over me. He'd been freed from prison, and now his freedom had been stolen again.

And this time, there'd be no reprieve.

"Let's make sure we're alone," Hemi whispered. "Stay close."

I grasped his hand as we checked under Eileen's desk, behind the sofa, and in a storage closet. We shuffled through the hall and cleared the breakroom, conference room, restroom, and closet. When we opened the front door, there was nothing on the stoop.

Hemi led us back to Eileen's desk. "There's no sign of a break in, so Fulton must've picked the lock."

"Unless Eileen let him in, they had a confrontation that ended with her shooting him, and she lied about what time she left." I bit my lip because I couldn't picture the frazzled mother of three shooting a man in the back.

He nodded. "If Fulton weren't shot in the back, I'd say self-defense or a confrontation was likely, but it appears someone sneaked up on him."

"Or he didn't come alone, and that person betrayed him." I shivered. "Call 911. I want to peek in Dad's filing cabinets while we have the chance." I also wanted to see if Fulton had a knife.

Uncertainty flickered in Hemi's eyes, but he opened the phone on Eileen's desk. I detoured to the breakroom and looked for dishwashing gloves under the sink. There weren't any, but I located a plastic baggie in a drawer. Slipping the baggie over my hand, I returned to Dad's office, and a lump rose in my throat.

Being careful not to step in the blood pooling around Fulton's body, I knelt beside him and pushed up his pant leg. Sure enough, an ankle sheath held a knife. Had Fulton been expecting danger? If so, why?

I peered into the filing cabinet—that contained tax records for the past seven years. Had Fulton been searching for the information Dad hadn't sent? I slid the drawer shut and opened the others. More business records. The bottom compartment held dusty extension cords.

I reopened the filing cabinet drawer to match the way we'd found it and observed details about the office. A drafting table was pushed against a wall. Closed mini blinds. Dad's computer was powered off. A desk with an empty outbox in the corner, a Rolodex, a container of pens and pencils, and our family picture from Rochelle's wedding.

Nothing out of the ordinary but a dead man.

I backed out of Dad's office and into the reception area where Hemi was hanging up the phone.

"What'd you find?" he asked.

"Fulton had a knife—just like Stan told us. Nothing appears out of place, and the filing cabinet drawer just has tax records."

"Maybe Fulton hid whatever he had for your dad in the tax records where most people would never think to look."

"Good thought. Let me check again." I returned to the filing cabinet, while trying to ignore the scent of blood permeating the office. I flipped through the files, but they were only tax records. I removed the bag from my hand, stuck it in my jacket pocket, and returned to the reception area. "Nothing. Maybe the killer took whatever Fulton had for Dad."

"Or Stan Stanton is wrong, and Fulton didn't have anything to give him."

I froze as another thought slammed into me. "Hemi, when we came in, we didn't see any vehicles parked in the lot—or on the street."

"You're right." He flipped through the Yellow Pages. "There are two cab companies in Richardville that Fulton could've used if he's staying at a motel there."

"But he was going on a road trip to Pennsylvania, so he had his own vehicle. Why pay for a cab?"

"That'd be a waste of money." He set the phonebook on the desk. "What if the killer took Fulton's vehicle?"

"Which would make sense if they came together, but otherwise, the killer would've most likely had his own vehicle and wouldn't have needed Fulton's."

"If Fulton was alone, he might've parked somewhere else to be less noticeable," Hemi said.

I considered this angle. "How would you feel about searching the neighborhood for vehicles with Illinois license plates?"

"I don't suppose you'll listen when I tell you that you should let the police investigate." His eyes glimmered with mischief.

"You supposed correctly."

"Then I'm in, but only after the detectives get here and tell us we're free to leave."

"Fair enough." I flipped through Eileen's Rolodex until I found Bruce Reynolds's contact information. "I want to know if Dad's foreman saw anything unusual today."

I punched in Bruce's number, but the answering machine picked up. His wife's cheery voice informed me they couldn't take my call but to leave my name and number, so I did. I hung up and faced Hemi. "I hope Detective Melchor doesn't think my dad had something to do with Fulton's murder."

Hemi grimaced. "I'd like to reassure you, since your parents haven't been seen for weeks, but Detective Girly Hands isn't a Guy Baxter fan."

Earlier this summer, after Detective Melchor had suspected my dad had killed Ross Garland, Hemi and I had nicknamed the prickly detective. Detective Melchor resented that I'd helped his department solve cases this summer, and even the fact that he was my friend Misty's stepfather didn't help my cause. His partner, Detective Jean Harrell, was fair and seemed to appreciate my input, though after what'd happened to my dad, I didn't trust her, or any cop, completely.

Sirens blared outside, so I opened the front door and let the sheriff's deputies inside. Another car roared into the parking lot. Detective Harrell entered as more deputies arrived and blue lights flashed. She wore a gray pantsuit, and dark circles rimmed her eyes. I guessed she was somewhere around fifty, but tonight she appeared older—and wearier—than I'd ever noticed.

"We have to stop meeting like this, Miss Baxter." She pointed at the chairs across from the sofa in the reception area. "Wait there, and don't leave until we've talked." She looked at Hemi. "You too, Mr. Miller."

"Yes, ma'am," he said.

We settled next to each other and watched as deputies swarmed in and out of the office.

"I wonder where Melchor is?" Hemi whispered.

I glanced at the door as it opened and expected to see Detective Melchor, but Sheriff Ralph Carter moseyed in instead. Gray flecked his dark hair, and a toothpick hung from his thin lips. His hawkish gaze swept the room before landing on Hemi and me.

Without a hint of friendliness in his expression, Hemi stood and extended his hand to the stocky man. "Sheriff Carter."

Interesting that the sheriff was here at all. During my adventures this summer, I'd yet to run into the man. His term was almost up, and since he wasn't running for re-election, word on the street was that he was burning vacation days and coasting toward retirement.

Sheriff Carter removed his toothpick with one hand and shook Hemi's with the other. "What're you doing here, Hemi?"

Was there a hint of annoyance in his tone, or was that Sheriff Carter's baseline?

"I was with Bobbi Sue when she came to check on her dad's office."

I rose. "I'm Bobbi Sue Baxter."

"I know." His face remained expressionless. Nothing in his tone indicated if this knowledge was good or bad. It simply existed. He fixed his attention on Hemi. "You telling me you two found the victim and called it in?"

"Yes, sir." Hemi glanced at me.

"Any idea who the victim is?"

"Morris Fulton," I said.

"What was he doing here?" Sheriff Carter focused on Hemi and didn't seem to care that I was standing there—or that this crime had taken place in *my* dad's office.

Hemi shifted. "We think he might've been attempting to locate Mr. Baxter."

"Really." Sheriff Carter turned his back, cutting me out of the conversation. "Guess he hadn't heard Guy Baxter disappeared."

"I guess not." Hemi clamped his mouth shut, and his jaw ticked.

"You given a statement?" Sheriff Carter asked Hemi.

"*We're* waiting to do that," I blurted before Hemi could answer.

"Good. Sit tight." Without looking at me, Sheriff Carter gave Hemi's shoulder a pat, put his toothpick back in his mouth, and ambled toward Dad's office.

Hemi and I sat, and I whispered, "How does he know you?"

"He's a bookstore customer. After he and his wife got divorced, he had his eye on my mother until she started dating Willis Brooks."

The edge of my mouth twitched because I couldn't picture the sheriff with Hemi's prim and proper mother. "I bet she found his toothpick irresistible."

He choked back a laugh as Detective Harrell approached us.

"Where's Detective Melchor?" I asked her. "I'm surprised he isn't here."

Detective Harrell removed her gloves. "He's on vacation." She took a notebook and pen out of her jacket pocket and sat on the sofa across from Hemi and me. "All right, Ms. Baxter, Mr. Miller. What happened this evening?"

Sheriff Carter ambled within earshot as I told her about Special Agent Erickson's visit a few days earlier, contacting Juanita St. James and her arrival, learning Morris Fulton had come to Wildcat Springs, and getting the tip from Stan Stanton that Fulton had been looking for my dad's office. "After we called my dad's business manager, Eileen, and found out she'd closed early and gone home, I thought we should check to see if Fulton left anything for my dad."

"I see," she said. "Do you have anything to add, Mr. Miller?"

"When we saw Mr. Fulton on the floor, I checked for a pulse, but we were careful not to disturb the scene."

"Thank you." She glanced over at Sheriff Toothpick, who was leaning against the wall and had his hairy arms folded across his chest. "Where were you this afternoon, Ms. Baxter?"

She was doing her job, but I resented the implication in her question. "I worked at Chuckie's Chicken until three. Then I went home to get ready for the picnic Hemi and I were planning in Sycamore Park." I glanced at him. "Misty Ambrose came over around three-thirty and was with me until a little before five when I left for Hemi's house." Hemi didn't need to know that I'd relied on her fashion advice and coaching.

She wrote in her notebook. "What about you, Mr. Miller?"

"I was at the library from about two to three o'clock. Then, I mowed my yard—and my neighbor's. They're on vacation this week, but my other neighbor, Mrs. Wilson, saw me and brought me lemonade. After that, I got cleaned up and packed for our picnic."

At least we both had alibis.

"Ms. Baxter, do you know where your parents went?" Detective Harrell asked.

Even though my dad hadn't been in town for over a month, was she seriously thinking of him as a suspect? "No." I set my jaw.

"Have they called you?"

"No." I glanced toward the sheriff, who still appeared to be listening.

"Did either of your parents ever mention Morris Fulton?" she asked.

"No. I'd never heard of him until the FBI agent mentioned him."

She wrote on her notepad. "Do you know how many people have keys to this office?"

"My parents, but they left them behind, and I used their set to get in this evening. Eileen Donahue and Bruce Reynolds have keys. I don't know about anyone else."

"Thank you. Now, just to clarify." Detective Harrell checked her notes. "Ms. St. James followed Fulton from Wabash Ridge, Illinois, to Wildcat Springs?"

I glanced at Hemi out of the corner of my eye, and he shifted and cleared his throat. "Juanita stopped in Wabash Ridge on her way to Wildcat Springs to see *me* because she knows I'm concerned about my parents and would like answers," I said. "Until she talked to Fulton's sister this morning, she had no idea he'd come here."

Detective Harrell glanced at Sheriff Toothpick. "I see."

But I wasn't sure she did. "I reached out to Juanita for information about Morris Fulton after Special Agent Erickson visited. I had no idea she'd come to Wildcat Springs and tell me my dad had helped clear Fulton's name—or that Fulton wanted to help my dad with other wrongful conviction cases."

"How long has she known about your parents' disappearing act?" Detective Harrell asked.

"I told her not long after it happened," I said.

"Uh-huh." Detective Harrell closed her notebook. "Where is Ms. St. James? I need to speak with her."

"She's looking for Fulton at Richardville motels. We're planning to meet back at my house," I said. "She intends to stay the night before heading back to Chicago."

She glanced at her watch. "You two are free to go, but I'll stop by your house later to speak with Ms. St. James. If you see her, tell her not to leave before I talk to her."

"Okay," I said—even though the situation didn't seem quite right. "But I have a question."

Sheriff Toothpick cleared his throat.

Detective Harrell gave a sideways glance at the sheriff. "Yes?"

"Do *you* have any idea why Special Agent Erickson wanted to talk to my dad and had questions about Morris Fulton?"

"No." She stood. "This is the first I've heard of it."

"Do you plan to contact him and find out why?" I asked.

"Yes." Annoyance crept into her tone. "Do you have his information?"

"I have a business card that you can have. It's at home."

"Thank you," she said. "I'll get it when I come talk to Ms. St. James."

I picked a smudge of nail polish from my cuticle. "Will you please let me know what you find out from Special Agent Erickson?"

She glanced at the sheriff. "I'll see you later, Ms. Baxter. You and Mr. Miller are free to go." She and Sheriff Carter returned to Dad's office.

Since we'd been dismissed, Hemi and I went outside where dusk was settling over the town.

"You asked me to join you on a picnic, and you get involved in a murder investigation," I said. "I'm so sorry."

"None of this is your fault." He took my hand and squeezed it. "But I'm glad we both have alibis."

"Me too. I don't like how Detective Harrell fixated on Juanita."

"That didn't sit well with me either, but she may've been trying to impress Sheriff Carter."

I hoped he was right.

Hemi glanced back at Dad's building. "Where do you want to look for Fulton's vehicle?"

"You don't have to spend your evening searching," I said. "I know this isn't what you had in mind."

"I don't care as long as I'm with you."

"Really?" My tummy fluttered at the intensity of his gaze.

"Yes, really. And there's no way I'd let you traipse through the dark alone looking for a vehicle when we don't know who murdered Fulton or where that person might be."

"Ever the gentleman."

"Thank you, but I want to know what happened too. The truth always matters, right?"

"It does." I held his gaze and fought the urge to kiss him because this wasn't the time or place, so I said, "Let's take a walk in this neighborhood and see what we find."

"All right." Hand in hand, we followed the alley until we reached Washington Street. The residential area had ranch-style houses in various states of upkeep. We passed kids playing basketball and tiptoed over a section of children's chalk drawings on the sidewalk.

We approached a yellow El Camino, but when we drew closer, I spotted an Indiana plate. Several houses had cars, trucks, and station wagons parked in driveways, but all the vehicles had Indiana registrations. When the street came to a T, Hemi and I turned right onto Willow Road.

Five red-brick townhouse apartments lined the opposite side of the street, and behind them was a small, wooded area. Several vehicles were parked in front of the building labeled *Willow Haven*, probably because of the large willow tree looming near the entrance.

"Let's stroll through this lot," I said.

We crossed the street and perused the lot. Each car had an Indiana plate, but a red GMC truck with a white panel was backed into the space next to the dumpster.

Hemi pointed as we got closer. "That truck has a front plate, so it's not registered in Indiana."

We approached the truck, and I wrinkled my nose at the sour odor wafting from the dumpster. Sure enough, the truck had an Illinois license plate.

"If this truck is Fulton's, he picked a good place to hide it because the residents probably assumed someone had a visitor." I peered through the window into the cab. On the bench seat was an atlas open to the Indiana map. "We need confirmation." I looked at the building behind me. Light streamed around the curtains in one unit, but the rest were dark. I took the plastic baggie from my jacket pocket, covered my hand, and opened the door. "It's our lucky day."

Hemi glanced around. "If we don't get caught."

I opened the glove compartment and pushed aside napkins and straws until I uncovered the registration paperwork. "This truck is Fulton's." I pawed through the glove compartment but only found the owner's manual. As I shut the truck door, a woman's angry voice made me jump.

"If you want my advice, you'll dump that pig boyfriend of yours because you're better off alone."

"Let's get out of here," Hemi whispered and shrank back against the dumpster.

A middle-aged woman with ramrod posture marched around the corner as her American Eskimo dog trotted ahead on a leash. "You don't need a man to be happy or to take care of you. I'm living proof," she said to a young brunette with drooped shoulders trudging beside her.

The young woman's face crumpled. "I don't want to talk about it," she wailed before bolting into her townhouse and slamming the door.

The fluffy white dog yapped and strained against the leash, as if it wanted to chase the younger woman and comfort her.

The middle-aged woman muttered a few expletives about men, and we'd almost escaped to the sidewalk when she stopped on the path leading to her apartment and looked between us and the truck. "You folks friends of the new guy?"

CHAPTER 5

THE MAN HATER and her canine companion eyed Hemi and me. She wore biker shorts and an Army green T-shirt with the logo: *Be all you can be.* She was committed to the military theme because even her dog's collar was camouflage print.

Was the new guy she'd mentioned Fulton? *Time to play dumb.* I issued a friendly smile as I walked away from the truck. "Have you seen him around?"

Please, give me a name.

"Not since this morning when he was unloading that truck after he signed the lease." She hitched her thumb at apartment five. "I told him he'd better not have the volume on the TV cranked up as loud as the last guy, or I'll see that Velda barks in the middle of the night as payback." She put a hand on her hip. "But I don't know if he's got a TV. Hardly had any stuff."

I glanced at Hemi, who was doing a fantastic job of looking innocent. "He's a considerate guy," I said. "I'm sure you don't have to worry even if he does."

"Good to know. He seemed nice enough—for a man—even though he has two last names instead of a proper first and last."

Hemi coughed and looked away.

"He can't help it if his parents weren't thinking about that, and at least they were more creative than my folks," she said. "You don't get much more generic than a name like Jane White. Didn't get much better when I married the loser who's now my ex. Took my maiden name back in the divorce though—and got this building and custody of my sweet girl Velda. Not a bad deal, if I say so myself. She keeps an eye on things for me." She bent to scratch the dog's head, and as she straightened, she brushed white hairs from her biker shorts.

I needed to get this conversation back on track before we heard Jane's life story. "It's funny. We'd heard Morris was headed for Pennsylvania, so we were surprised he settled in Wildcat Springs." I paused to see if his name got a reaction.

Jane shrugged. "Signed a six-month lease and paid the first month's rent in cash. Good enough for me, so I didn't ask questions. You folks have a nice evening." She looked back and forth between us, tugged on Velda's leash, and disappeared inside.

"Didn't see that news coming," I whispered.

"Your talent for stretching the truth worries me."

"I prefer to think of it as information extraction."

"Whatever you have to tell yourself."

My tummy fluttered when I met his warm gaze. "We need to figure out why Fulton told his sister he was going on a road trip to Pennsylvania but signed a six-month lease in Wildcat Springs."

"Want to see if he left his townhouse door unlocked too?" Hemi asked.

I elbowed him. "I'm corrupting you."

Hemi followed me to the door. "Don't remind me."

Once more, I covered my hand with the baggie and tried the door—that opened.

"For a guy who was wrongly convicted, he was pretty trusting to leave everything unlocked," Hemi muttered.

"A lot of people around here do—but my family never has."

"I don't either."

We stepped into the galley kitchen with harvest gold appliances and orange and brown linoleum. A grocery sack sat on the counter. Moving through the kitchen into the living room, I wrinkled my nose at the musty smell and came to an empty room with shaggy tan carpet. A narrow staircase led to a bedroom with an inflated air mattress, a portable TV/radio, backpack, and a suitcase.

Hemi used his shirt to cover his hand while he opened the suitcase. "Just clothes and sheets for the air mattress—no surprises."

With my hand covered, I unzipped the backpack. It contained a paperback novel, a Bible, notebook, and pens. I flipped through the novel and Bible, but no papers were tucked between the pages. The notebook was empty.

I zipped the backpack and went to the bathroom where I flicked on the light, but there was only a toiletry case on the counter. Shutting off the light, I rejoined Hemi. "Nothing in his luggage indicates that he came here intending to stay. Everything is logical for a road trip where he was visiting a friend—not moving into an unfurnished apartment."

"Then we need to figure out what happened between Fulton leaving Illinois yesterday afternoon and signing that lease this morning."

Hemi glanced out the window. "We should bounce before the detectives—or Fulton's killer shows up."

We passed back through the kitchen, but this time, an envelope wedged under the grocery sack on the kitchen counter caught my attention. "Hold on." I put the baggie back over my hand and picked up the envelope addressed to Fulton. My eyes widened.

"What?"

"The return address is Dad's construction office—and this is his writing." I slid the letter out and held it so we could both read.

Morris,

I understand your need to pay it forward, and I had a case come to my attention that you can help with. A guy named Errol Danforth has been in prison for several years for armed robbery, and when I started digging, I didn't like what I found. I'll send you photocopies of everything I have—expect a file in the mail in the next week or so after I get to the courthouse to see what else I can find.

Take care,

Guy

I pointed at the postmark on the envelope. "Mom and Dad left on June nineteenth—three days *after* he mailed this letter," I said. "I bet Dad didn't have a chance to get to the courthouse or send the file to Fulton before they fled."

"But we don't know where Errol Danforth is from or what courthouse your dad was even talking about. It could be anywhere."

"If Dad thought he could get to the courthouse within a week of writing this note, then it can't be too far. It's not like he investigated full time."

"It's possible he meant the Richard County Courthouse," Hemi said. "If Fulton went there himself, he might've found something important to show your dad."

I put the letter back in the envelope and placed it on the counter underneath the sack. "And that could be why he decided to stick around."

After Hemi and I had left Fulton's townhouse, we'd decided I should get my car so we could drive separately to my house to meet Juanita. As we entered the kitchen through the back door, my gray tabby, Nita, slinked in from the dining room and rubbed around my legs.

"Hey, sweet kitty." I dropped my purse and keys on the counter. "What a day."

"No kidding." Hemi bent and patted Nita's head while she purred and waved her tail.

"I know we just found a man dead, but I can't shake the feeling that another shoe is about to drop."

"You could be feeling burdened about Fulton." Hemi stood. "Seeing a man exonerated only to be murdered is tragic—and the injustice is disturbing. Not to mention how awful it was to find him."

"You're right—it was something I'll never unsee." I picked up my cat and cuddled her, but she squirmed.

"Now what?"

I freed Nita. "Let's see if my dad left anything about Danforth in his office." I led Hemi down the hall, but the bell rang, so I pointed him to the living room and veered to the door. "Hey, Juanita."

She breezed into the foyer. "Fulton stayed at a fleabag motel on the north side of Richardville last night but checked out this morning. The owner let me pay for an hour to search the room, but I didn't find a thing but cockroaches and a bedspread that could use a good washing." She grimaced, took off her jacket, and tossed it over her suitcase. "Did you have any luck?"

"I wouldn't call it luck," I said.

"Because?"

I put her luggage at the foot of the stairs and motioned for her to follow me to the living room. "Unfortunately, we found Fulton shot dead in Dad's construction office."

Juanita gasped. "Give a woman some warning before you drop a bombshell like that. Wow." She collapsed onto the couch. "Poor man. What do you know? And why were you at Guy's office?" She eyed Hemi who was sitting in Dad's recliner.

I told her about the tip from Stan Stanton, finding Fulton, and how we'd discovered Fulton had leased a townhouse at Willow Haven. I shared that we'd snooped inside and found the letter from my dad with the mention of Errol Danforth's case.

"We don't know if Mr. Baxter made it to the courthouse or sent the file because the letter was postmarked a few days before they left," Hemi said.

Juanita nodded. "If your dad didn't mail the file, that could be why Fulton stopped in Wildcat Springs and broke into the office."

"Right," I said. "And by the way, Detective Harrell is coming to talk to you."

Juanita shrugged. "Doesn't surprise me. Since you told her I visited Fulton's hometown this morning, she may be wondering if I learned anything helpful."

I hoped Sheriff Toothpick wouldn't come with Detective Harrell.

A rap sounded on the door, and I jumped up and answered, expecting Detective Harrell. But Bruce Reynolds stood on the porch instead. He was around thirty-five, with a blond buzz cut and a tan from working outside at construction sites, and he was wearing jeans and a Metallica T-shirt.

"I got your message," he said. "But before I could call back, my phone started ringing off the hook with people wondering what was going on at your dad's office. I drove over and found the sheriff and cops swarming, and they told me someone had been shot. Then, the lady detective grilled me about where I'd been all afternoon and evening."

"I'm sorry." I sagged against the doorframe. "Come in."

"I can't. I gotta get home, but I wanted to check on you." He shoved his hands into his pockets. "I was with my crew all day and was only alone on my drive home."

"Did you stop at the office or talk to Eileen today?" I asked.

"No. I didn't have time." The crease between his eyebrows deepened. "That lady detective kept asking me if I knew anything about Morris Fulton. I swear I've never even heard of the guy." He leaned closer. "You're going to poke around, right? I'm worried about being tapped for this when I had nothing to do with it. I got a wife and kids to take care of."

"I understand," I said. "I want to get to the bottom of this too, so you'd better believe I'm going to investigate."

He blew out a breath. "I keep hoping your dad will roll back into town, and everything will go back to normal. I've been trying to keep things running, but my life would be a lot easier if he'd come home."

"Mine too. I appreciate your hard work, and I'm sorry I don't have answers," I said.

He glanced at his watch. "I've gotta scoot, but if I think of anything else, I'll let you know. Keep me in the loop."

"Will do." I closed the door and headed to the living room but laughed at Juanita and Hemi lurking around the corner. "Eavesdropping?"

Juanita narrowed her eyes. "I don't trust that guy."

"Why?" I asked.

After Dad's business partner had set him up for a crime, he'd been cautious about who he'd hired. He'd vetted Bruce and Eileen well and did background checks on the construction workers he hired.

"My gut—and I'm almost never wrong." Juanita narrowed

her eyes. "The fact that he's overly worried about a false accusation doesn't feel right."

The doorbell rang—again.

"I live in Grand Central Station," I muttered as I walked to the door. This time, Detective Harrell was waiting on the porch —alone.

"Was Bruce Reynolds just here?" she asked as I led her into the living room. "I thought I saw him leaving."

"Yes."

"Why?"

Did she suspect Bruce too? "He wanted to check on me after he heard what happened at Dad's office."

"Got it." She crossed over to Juanita and introduced herself. "I have some questions about Morris Fulton, Ms. St. James." She perched on the couch opposite Juanita.

"Go ahead." Juanita crossed her long legs. "Do you mind if Bobbi Sue and Hemi stay?"

"Might as well," Detective Harrell said. "If I say *no,* they'll eavesdrop, or you'll fill them in later."

"With good reason." Juanita crossed her arms. "Bobbi Sue's a smart young lady who'll make a great journalist, and her friend is sharp too."

Detective Harrell remained stone-faced, opened her notepad, and took a pen from her jacket pocket. "Why'd you visit Wabash Ridge, Illinois, this morning?"

"Monday evening, Bobbi Sue left a message saying that FBI Special Agent Cole Erickson had visited her and asked about Morris Fulton, who'd been in the same prison as her father. If you're not aware, Guy Baxter was set up for murder, wrongfully convicted, and served time until I was able to find evidence to exonerate him."

"I'm familiar with the story," Detective Harrell said.

"No doubt." Juanita's tone was cool as she met the detective's gaze. "Morris Fulton was also wrongly convicted, and Guy found evidence to exonerate him. When Bobbi Sue told me the FBI agent mentioned Fulton, I attempted to visit him this morning on my way here to see if he knew why or how this could be connected to Guy. I had vacation time, and until now, I haven't been able to help Bobbi Sue figure out what's going on with her parents."

Detective Harrell scribbled some notes. "What'd you find when you visited Wabash Ridge?"

Juanita told Detective Harrell about Fulton leaving for Pennsylvania with the intent to stop in Wildcat Springs to see my dad. She shared that Fulton wanted to help Dad with another possible wrongful conviction case.

"You believe Fulton came to Wildcat Springs not realizing Guy is out of town?" Detective Harrell asked.

"Yes," Juanita said. "Based on everything his sister Lucia said, he had no idea."

"But he decided to stay in Wildcat Springs for a while," I blurted.

"And you know this because?" Detective Harrell eyed me.

"Fulton's vehicle wasn't parked at Dad's office, so we searched the neighborhood and found a truck with Illinois plates in the Willow Haven parking lot. The landlady, Jane White, told us he'd signed a six-month lease earlier today." I stopped myself from telling the story of our snooping in the townhouse because they'd find the letter soon enough.

Detective Harrell compressed her lips. "By *we,* you mean…?"

"Bobbi Sue and me." Hemi met her gaze.

Detective Harrell focused on Juanita. "Where were you?"

"Richardville," she said. "Like I told you, I was checking motels for Fulton."

Detective Harrell jotted something in her notebook. "Miss Baxter, I realize you've been helpful this summer, but I do *not* need further assistance with this investigation. Do you understand?"

"Yes, ma'am." *And you're welcome.*

"The same goes for you, Mr. Miller. Am I clear?"

"Yes, ma'am." His jaw ticked.

Detective Harrell directed her gaze back at Juanita. "I have more questions."

"Go ahead." Juanita shifted.

"You're a busy woman, and yet you took time off work to help Bobbi Sue. What makes you think the Baxters didn't take a long vacation, and you aren't just wasting time?"

"Nicki was my college roommate," Juanita said. "She'd make weekend plans on Monday and confirm multiple times throughout the week. She finished her papers and projects early. There's no way she'd go on vacation without planning for months."

Detective Harrell looked at me. "Do you agree?"

"Yes, and Mom wouldn't want to worry Rochelle, Grandma, and me by taking off on vacation unannounced, especially since my sister's pregnant. We're trying not to stress her out because she already had one miscarriage and is terrified of having another," I said. "Mom and Dad left because of an emergency."

Detective Harrell shifted. "Ms. St. James, do you own a firearm?"

Hemi and I exchanged glances.

"I do not." Juanita's tone remained even and calm. "I live and work in Chicago, and Illinois has restrictive gun laws."

"When did you arrive in Wildcat Springs?" Detective Harrell asked.

"Today."

"What time?"

"Late afternoon."

Detective Harrell wrote in her notebook. "Give me a ballpark time."

Juanita appeared to hesitate for a moment. "Around 3:45."

She'd found Hemi and me in the park around 5:30. If she'd come to the house at 3:45, I'd have been home with Misty, but she'd told us that she'd come here, hadn't found me, and then she'd gone to Chuckie's and Tate's Place before Misty had told her I was at the park.

Had Juanita lied? And if so, why?

"Where'd you go when you got into town?" Detective Harrell asked.

"I attempted to find Bobbi Sue at the places where I knew she might be. Her home. Then Chuckie's and Tate's Place, where her friend Misty told me Bobbi Sue was on a date with Hemi at Sycamore Park."

Detective Harrell scribbled on her notepad. "Did you go to Guy Baxter's construction office?"

"I've told you everything I know about Morris Fulton." Juanita stood and lifted her chin. "And I'm done answering questions."

CHAPTER 6

DETECTIVE HARRELL BLINKED AT JUANITA. "I see." She stood and closed her notebook. "I'll be in touch. Ms. Baxter, do you have Special Agent Erickson's business card?"

"Yes. Give me a minute, please." I headed for the stairs while Detective Harrell followed and waited in the foyer. With shaky legs, I trudged upstairs to my room.

What was Juanita hiding? Had she confronted Fulton at Dad's office? Or worse—no. I couldn't go there.

The card was on my desk, wedged under my copy of *To Kill a Mockingbird*. Shaking away my confusion about Juanita, I wrote the contact information onto a notepad before I went downstairs and handed the card to Detective Harrell.

"Thank you." She tucked it into her pocket. "Remember, we have this investigation covered."

"I understand." A knot formed in my gut as I locked the door behind her. Was Juanita not the honorable woman I believed her to be? If I couldn't have faith in the person who'd helped exonerate my dad, then who *could* I trust?

"Please tell me you copied down that FBI agent's information," Juanita said as I returned to the living room and sat on the couch.

Hemi appeared as annoyed as I felt.

"Yes." I gritted my teeth. "Do you mind explaining what's going on? I was here with Misty at 3:45, so there are a few issues with your timeline."

"I didn't lie about coming to the house," she said. "I just didn't tell you that I went to your dad's office first."

"Why?" Hemi demanded. "Because you ran into Fulton and didn't want to incriminate yourself?"

"Nope." She opened her messenger bag and withdrew a small manila envelope. "This." She handed it to me. "Open it."

The envelope jangled, so I tipped it over, and two keys slid out. One was a regular door key, and the other was a metal tube meant for a safe lock. I held up the safe key. "I need more info."

"Read the note." Juanita pointed at the envelope.

I removed the paper, and the handwriting was Dad's. "Dear Juanita," I read, "If anything happens to Nicki and me, I want you to have access to my construction office safe. I've been digging into wrongful conviction cases, so that's where I'll put copies of evidence that might make the wrong people mad. There's nothing yet, but I want a backup plan. The safe is underneath the floor in the hall closet, and I've enclosed an office key too." I looked up from the note. "I never knew about that safe. How long have you had these?"

"Seven—eight years."

"You didn't want to tell Detective Harrell that you went to the office to check the safe and incriminate yourself," Hemi said.

"Correct. No one was there—not even the office manager."

"She'd left early because her kid was sick," I said. "Did you find anything in the safe?"

Juanita shook her head. "Not a single thing."

My head spun as I tried to sort the details. "How long were you there?"

"Ten minutes or so. I admit that when I found the safe

empty, I poked through your dad's files but didn't find anything unusual there either."

"But your fingerprints will be all over the office," Hemi said.

"Unfortunately." She winced. "I wasn't trying to hide my visit. As far as I'm concerned, I had permission. If Eileen had been there, I would've shown her the letter and checked the safe. After I finished, I locked up and left. I couldn't have missed Fulton and the killer by much, but I swear I didn't see anyone. I told the detective everything I know about Fulton, so I don't feel bad about sending her on her way."

Though I would've preferred Juanita being forthcoming about her timeline sooner, there was no point in worrying about that now. I stood. "Let's check Dad's home office for the Danforth file."

"Good idea." Hemi got up.

I led them to the office. "I'll start with the floor safe here because I didn't know I was supposed to be looking for a file when I searched it after Mom and Dad left." I threw the rug aside, knelt beside the safe, and opened it. I sorted through the envelopes with our birth certificates and Mom and Dad's actual IDs and looked up. "Nothing on Danforth."

I secured the safe, opened the bottom filing cabinet next to Dad's desk, and flipped through the folders. They contained Mom and Dad's homeowner's insurance policy, their will, loan paperwork, and medical insurance records. I tried the middle drawer, but it held Mom's substitute lesson plans and teacher's editions of textbooks. In the top drawer, I found file folders stuffed with newspaper clippings, so I removed them.

"These might be something." I handed a stack of folders to Juanita and another to Hemi before taking one for myself. I settled at Dad's desk while Hemi and Juanita took opposite ends of the couch. While we combed through the files, the room was quiet except for paper rustling and the occasional squeak from the desk chair.

The first folder I checked contained clippings about UFO sightings, which didn't surprise me. Dad loved anything conspiracy related, and he'd even formed a club with a couple of guys from our church. After glancing at the clippings, I put the folder aside and moved to the next one.

Juanita looked up from her folder. "So far, I've found articles about the JFK assassination and an article about a man who wrote a book about the moon landing being fake." She held out the clipping about the book.

"I found a folder on Roswell." Hemi lifted a file from the coffee table. "Do you think your dad would mind if I borrowed it?"

I grinned at Hemi—who'd once dreamed of being a ufologist. "Nope. He'd be happy for you to read it, and thrilled if you talked to him about it—when he comes home."

"Thanks." He set the folder aside and continued through his remaining stack.

I flipped through another file about Elvis sightings and tossed it onto the discard pile. Years ago, I'd been convinced that my friend Misty's neighbor had been Elvis, and my mistake had even inspired the man to become an impersonator.

On to the next folder. "Bigfoot," I muttered as I tossed it onto the desk. I grabbed the last folder and read *Errol Danforth* on the tab. "Got it." I found handwritten notes on a yellow legal pad and a folded paper.

Juanita moved the files from her lap to the coffee table and stood beside me. "What's your dad have on Danforth?"

"Not much." I skimmed Dad's notes. "A jury convicted Errol Danforth of armed robbery in April 1986 here in Richard County. There were eyewitnesses, but Dad must not have names because he has the words *witness names* with a question mark.

He also wrote, 'Did someone frame Danforth?'" I looked up. "I wonder what evidence made him ask that."

"Tomorrow we should check court records for information about the evidence presented at the trial," Juanita said. "What's on the other paper?"

"A letter." I unfolded it and held it so they could read it too.

Dear Mr. Baxter,

My name is Errol Danforth, and I'm an inmate at Wilford Correctional Facility. In April 1986, I was found guilty of the armed robbery of a convenience store in Richardville. I've heard you help people convicted of crimes they didn't commit. I didn't rob that store, even though the clerk and another customer testified that I did. I was at home that night watching TV, but someone stole my gun sometime before the robbery and used it that night to set me up. I swear someone paid the clerk and customer to lie, and the store didn't have security cameras. Would you please look into my case? If you can't help, I understand, but the system worked against me—like it did for you. If you can, please write or visit me, and I'll tell the rest of my story.

Respectfully,
Errol Danforth

I put the letter back into the folder. "Now I understand why Dad thought someone framed Danforth—if he's telling the truth."

"It's possible your dad gets a lot of requests like this," Hemi said. "Not all of them would be legit."

"Right." I bit my lip. "Even if Danforth is being honest, we don't know *why* someone would do that to him."

"Knowing your dad, he investigated enough to realize Danforth wasn't playing him," Juanita said. "Otherwise, he wouldn't have mentioned the case to Morris Fulton."

I grabbed the stack of my parents' mail I'd collected and sorted through it. "No letters from Danforth. Maybe Dad went to see him in prison instead of writing."

"He might've, but he'd have to go through the visitor approval process first. That can take time," Juanita said. "Come to think of it, what if Fulton dug around while he was here, found something substantial to help exonerate Danforth, and that's why he decided to stay?"

"If that's true, and Danforth was framed, then whoever did it might've been tipped off about Fulton's investigation." Hemi met my eyes.

I dropped the mail stack onto the desk. "And that might be why Fulton's dead."

CHAPTER 7

HEMI, Juanita, and I sat in silence until she said, "Let's see if we can get approval to visit Danforth at Wilford Correctional. As I said, though, that process can take a while."

"Are you sure that's a good idea?" Hemi asked. "We could end up dead like Fulton."

"I'll do it myself. You and Bobbi Sue don't have to be involved." She didn't hide the annoyance in her tone.

"I want to go." I faced Juanita. "It's a chance for me to learn from you, and besides, the whole town will hear that I found Fulton and will assume that I'm investigating."

"But they don't know about the Danforth connection." Hemi folded his arms.

"We don't know if Fulton put in a visitation request to see Danforth, and we certainly don't know if Fulton's nosing into Danforth's case is why he was shot," Juanita said. "We're just speculating."

"Fine. Do what you have to do." Hemi glanced at me with concern in his eyes. "Do you think your grandma would know anything about Danforth since it's a local case?"

"Probably." Grandma Spearman had worked for the sheriff's department before retiring, and she had sources who'd helped us before. However, I had a feeling he was hoping Grandma would convince me to stay away from this investigation. "It's time we loop her in." I checked my watch. "But it's late."

"Let's get some rest," Juanita said. "We'll talk to your grandma tomorrow morning before we go to the courthouse."

The next morning, the scents of bacon and coffee awakened me from a fitful sleep, and I sat up in bed and blinked. Were Mom and Dad home? I grabbed my robe, walked into my slippers, and joined Juanita in the kitchen.

"I'm the worst hostess ever," I said. "I should be making *you* breakfast."

Juanita turned from the stove. "I'm no gourmet chef, but I can make eggs, bacon, and toast, so that's what we're getting. I couldn't sleep, so I made myself useful."

"Thank you." I grabbed a mug and poured some coffee since I didn't always bother to make a pot for myself. Then, I set the table.

Juanita brought the eggs, bacon platter, and toast slices to the table. I offered a blessing and threw in a petition for divine help with this case and protection for Mom and Dad.

I'd barely said "amen" when Juanita dumped a scoopful of eggs onto my plate and asked, "Are you going to marry Hemi?"

I took a sip of coffee—and another. "You don't pull any punches, do you?"

"You're awfully young for marriage when you have a career to consider."

"Hold on," I said. "I haven't even answered your question."

"Well?"

"I don't know. I like him. He's a great guy, and we became friends when I was working in his mom's bookstore. She didn't like that because Hemi was engaged, so she found an excuse to fire me. And then she fired me from the newspaper she runs too."

"What happened to his fiancée?" She scooped eggs onto her plate and took a bite.

"They decided they weren't right for each other." I broke a bacon strip in half. "Honestly, they didn't break up that long ago, so at first, I wasn't sure if yesterday's picnic was even a real date. But now I think it was."

"It was."

"How do you know?"

"By the way he looks at you—and because of how protective he is."

I pushed eggs around my plate.

"How does he feel about you wanting to be an investigative reporter?" She sipped her coffee.

"We haven't talked about it."

"Why not?"

"Because we're not at that relationship stage."

"He is." She ate another bite of eggs.

"How do you know? You're not a mind reader."

"No," she said. "But I observe behavior and know when a young man is smitten. What I'm trying to figure out is how *you* feel, because I don't want you to derail your career for the wrong guy."

"No one could accuse you of not putting your cards on the table." I forced eggs into my mouth, even though my appetite had vanished.

She dropped her fork onto her plate. "Bobbi Sue, do you really want to be an investigative reporter?"

I swallowed. "Yes."

"Well, I have my doubts because your actions are speaking louder than your words."

"How do you figure?"

"You never asked for my help getting an internship," she said. "Instead, you opted to spend the summer in Wildcat Springs working at the local greasy spoon."

I bristled. "I started out working in a bookstore and for a newspaper, and I've been writing freelance articles for *Hoosier* magazine."

"When your other jobs didn't work out, why didn't you ask me for help?"

"With Mom and Dad leaving suddenly, I've been dealing with a lot, so that's not fair."

"Have you ever considered you chose to stay here this summer because deep down, it's what you want?"

I jumped up and grabbed the coffee pot. "That's ridiculous. I can't wait to get out of here and live in a city."

"Then why are you getting involved with someone who'll keep you here?"

"Hemi's moving to Fort Wayne at the end of the summer." I topped off my coffee. He got a job teaching high school because his mother fired him from the bookstore after he refused to get back together with his fiancée."

"As glad as I am to hear he's getting away from his controlling mother, there's still a problem." Juanita squeezed the bridge of her nose. "If you marry him, you're marrying his family—including his manipulative mother."

"I know. That's why I'm not certain about him! You think I haven't noticed his overprotectiveness? That I haven't considered how he'll feel if I'm investigating dangerous situations?"

"I wasn't sure."

"Now you can be," I spat out. "I've thought of it."

She crossed her arms. "You can yell all you want, but you're not upset at me."

That much was true. "Are you happy with your life?" I asked quietly as I returned to the table.

"Yes." She blinked at me. "Why?"

"Are you ever sorry you didn't get married and have a family?"

"No. All I ever dreamed of being is a reporter. I didn't want children, although having a husband would be nice. But I haven't found a man willing to put up with me."

"Let's say you'd found a man and changed your mind about having kids. Would that have ruined your career?"

"A family wouldn't have ruined my career, but it might've forced me to take a less intense job," she said. "I'd be less willing to put myself in danger if I knew I had a husband and children waiting for me at home."

"That's what I thought."

"And that's what you're going to have to decide for yourself," she said. "Nobody else can make that call. Just be certain it's a decision you can live with in thirty years."

"I was about to drive out to see you," Grandma Spearman said as she opened her front door later that morning. "For once, you thought of your widowed grandmother and saved her the trip, although I can't give you too much credit because you should've been here last night."

Uh-oh. If this was the beginning of the guilt trip, then Hemi, Juanita, and I were in for an arduous journey.

She flicked her gaze to Juanita. "What're *you* doing here?"

"Nice to see you too, Mrs. Spearman." Juanita lifted her chin. "I'm helping Bobbi Sue figure out what's going on with Nicki and Guy."

"It's about time you solved the mystery of why that son-in-law of mine dragged my daughter off to goodness knows where," Grandma muttered. "I see the asparagus spear is in on the action too. Well, come on in." She stomped inside, motioning for us to follow.

Juanita shot an incredulous look at me, and mouthed, "Asparagus spear?"

I shook my head. Hemi was thin, but only Grandma had the nerve to refer to him as a vegetable to his face, which he thought was funny.

Hemi stopped and hugged Grandma. "You look pretty in that blouse."

"This old thing?" She smoothed her pink blouse that she'd paired with a skirt. You're such a sweetie." She patted his cheek. "Have you eaten breakfast?"

"Yes," we said in unison.

"Good. I don't feel like cooking, so you would've gotten shredded wheat or bran—without milk because I finished it off this morning." She pointed at her couch, encased in a plastic protector. "Sit. I have a feeling this could take a while." She smoothed her permed hair that was free from a single strand of gray.

"Did you hear about the murder at Dad's construction office?" I asked as Juanita, Hemi, and I lined up on the couch.

"Why do you think I said you should've been here last night?" She plopped into her recliner and folded her arms. "Once again, Judy Beeson scooped me because she heard it from her niece whose best friend's husband works for the sheriff's department."

"I'm sorry," I said.

"You should be. I can be valuable in these investigations, but when you're old, people forget about you." Grandma huffed. "Are you here because you finally realized you needed my help?"

Pretty much. I bit back the thought before it flew out of my mouth.

"Mrs. Spearman, were you aware that your son-in-law investigated wrongful convictions and attempted to find evidence to exonerate prisoners?" Juanita asked.

"You get right to the point, don't you?" Grandma asked.

Her comment was so much like mine earlier that morning that I cringed. Was I becoming Grandma Spearman?

Juanita didn't respond but stared at Grandma as if she refused to be intimidated. "Did you know?"

"No. But I'm not surprised that Guy kept that from me," Grandma said. "I'm not happy with Nicki though."

"Your daughter isn't the type to break her husband's confidence."

"I'm aware." Grandma lifted her chin.

"Did Guy ever mention Errol Danforth?" Juanita asked.

"No," Grandma said. "Why?"

I told Grandma what we'd learned about Morris Fulton, Dad's suspicions that Danforth had been framed, and the plan to send Fulton more information about Danforth's case before he and Mom left town. "We think Fulton came to check on Dad because he never heard from him, but when he got here, he found something important about Danforth and—"

"That's what got him killed," Grandma said.

"Right." I shifted, and the couch's plastic cover crinkled. "We don't think Dad had a chance to visit Danforth in prison or the courthouse before he and Mom left."

Grandma tapped her chin. "I remember that trial. There were folks who couldn't believe Danforth knocked over a convenience store, but others weren't surprised because he could be a hothead. If memory serves, the case hinged on the clerk and a customer identifying Danforth."

"That's right," I said. "Do you remember their names?"

"No." Grandma shook her head. "I've slept since then."

"Is there anything else you can recall?" Juanita asked.

Grandma drummed her fingers on the recliner's arm. "Danforth worked at Richardville Paint Factory, and I remember some kerfluffle happened at that place."

"You mean *kerfuffle*?" I asked.

"I like my word better, but this one thinks she knows everything since she's been to college." She hitched her thumb at me, but then her eyes got a faraway look. "I have an idea, but I need to do some digging. Run along, and I'll get back with you when I have something." Grandma shot to her feet and made a shooing motion.

"What is it?" I asked.

"I'll get back with you when I have something." She popped a hand onto her hip. "Are you losing your hearing? I've told you not to play the music so loud in your car."

"My hearing is fine. I can't believe you're leaving us hanging." I glanced at Hemi, and the traitor had a little too much amusement on his face.

"Believe it." She lifted her chin. "Right now, the less you know, the better."

"Let's head to the courthouse." Juanita stood and picked up her messenger bag. "And didn't you tell me your sister works at a shop in downtown Richardville?"

"Yes." I peeled my legs from the couch and got up. "She's working today."

"Good," Juanita said. "I'd love to see her after we go to the courthouse."

Why was Juanita deferring to Grandma?

"Excellent idea. Rochelle will be thrilled to see you, and if she hasn't already heard what happened at your dad's office, you'd better tell her before somebody else does." Grandma opened the front door, and for a second, I thought she'd kick us in the pants on the way out.

"Nice to see you again, Mrs. Spearman," Juanita said as we stepped into the heat.

"I'll be in touch." She looked at Hemi. "And you, young man, keep an eye on my granddaughter."

"Yes ma'am." Hemi clasped my hand. "I intend to."

"Good." Grandma slammed the door in our faces.

"What just happened?" I asked as we walked to my car.

"Your grandma may be protecting a source," Juanita said.

I unlocked the door. "But—"

"She probably knows someone who might have information that could help, but she suspects that person won't talk to all of us. Let her nose around and tell us when she's ready. That's more productive in the long run."

"You're right." Her deference was a strategic move, but I sighed as I got into the car.

Why did my life have to be so complicated?

CHAPTER 8

LATER THAT MORNING, Hemi, Juanita, and I entered the Richard County Courthouse, a three-story limestone building in the center of downtown Richardville. Inside the lobby, the terrazzo floor gleamed with black and gold specks, and marble wainscoting lined the walls.

Juanita paused next to the elevator and studied the directory. "We need the basement." She jabbed the call button, and when the bronze-colored doors slid open, we stepped inside and rode down. The doors parted, revealing a young woman with poufy bangs sitting behind an oak desk.

"Good morning," she said in a grating, mouse-like voice. "How may I help you?" She adjusted her oversized glasses, and when she looked at Hemi, I swore she thrust out her chest.

"We'd like to see the case files and court transcripts for the State of Indiana versus Errol Danforth," Juanita said. "April 1986."

Mousy Voice stood and squared her shoulders. "Our files are on microfilm." In her tight pants, she pranced around the desk and opened a door. Inside the closet-like space, a microfilm reader sat on a table with a chair in front of it. "Go on in, and I'll get the rolls." She trotted through the doorway behind her desk.

Juanita pointed to the chair. "Do the honors, Bobbi Sue."

I sat, and after Mousy Voice returned with the film rolls, she shot a longing gaze at Hemi before leaving us alone. He closed the door behind her, and I chose the roll with the court transcripts and loaded it into the reader.

"Skim through the prosecution's case for any details that stand out." Juanita took a notebook and pen from her messenger bag.

"Be on the lookout for the eyewitnesses' names," Hemi added.

I pressed the button to advance the film and skimmed the first page. "Let me know if I move too fast."

We read the prosecutor's opening argument in silence. The first witness was Detective Harrell, who testified about finding Danforth's gun with his fingerprints. No other prints were found on the gun. I advanced the film. "Here it is. The first eyewitness was Barnaby Feaster."

Hemi cocked his head. "That name sounds familiar, but I can't remember why."

"Because it sounds like a character from a Charles Dickens novel?" I asked.

Hemi chuckled. "It sure does."

Juanita scrawled on her notepad as we read silently. Barnaby had stopped at the convenience store for milk and was paying when a man matching Errol Danforth's description came in and pointed a gun at the clerk. According to Feaster, Danforth wore a bandana—like a cowboy. However, he recognized Danforth because of his skinny build, the bald spot on his head, and the getaway car—a silver Cutlass Supreme. He also testified the man wasn't wearing gloves.

The next eyewitness was the clerk—Oliver Hoffman. He confirmed Danforth's identity based on the car, eyes, and voice.

He caught a few matching numbers on Danforth's license plate as he drove away.

I turned to Juanita and Hemi. "If Danforth was set up, then were all three guys in on it? The person who played Danforth and the eyewitnesses?"

"Don't forget there could be another person pulling the strings," Juanita said.

Hemi leaned against the wall. "Or Danforth did rob the convenience store, and he was desperate to get out of prison and thought your dad could help."

So much about this situation wasn't adding up. "It's suspicious that the store's security cameras weren't working."

"Useful if you want to frame an innocent man." Juanita wrote in her notebook.

"I have an idea," Hemi said. "Did either of you bring the newspaper article with Morris Fulton's picture?"

"Yep." Juanita took the file folder from her bag and gave it to him.

Hemi opened the door and disappeared, but we heard him say, "I don't know if you're allowed to tell me, but did this man ask to see the case files and transcripts we're looking at?"

"Nice work, Hemi," Juanita murmured. "He'll have her eating out of his hand in no time."

I made a vomiting motion, and Juanita chuckled.

"Ummm, no, that guy didn't," Mousy Voice said. "Hey, has anyone ever told you that you look *just like* Matt Dillon?"

"You think?" Hemi scoffed. "That's nice of you to say."

I pictured Hemi blushing, glanced at Juanita, and rolled my eyes.

"Called it." She snickered.

"I'm Krystal—with a K," Mousy Voice drawled.

"Hemi," he said. "Did anyone else request the microfilm from this case lately?"

"Actually, there *was* a guy a couple of weeks ago. Pretty buff. Kinda grumpy." She paused. "Oh, and he had some tattoos."

That could describe Dad.

"Did you catch his name?" Hemi asked.

"No, I'm sorry. Unlike you, he wasn't very friendly, and he wasn't a journalist I'd seen before. We get a lot of the same reporters in here."

Juanita chuckled, but I was out of eye rolls and going to ralph if I didn't nip this in the bud.

I grabbed my wallet from my purse and flipped to our family picture from Rochelle's wedding. When I approached Krystal's desk, her face clouded as I held out the photo. "Is this the man you saw?" I pointed at Dad.

"No." She squinted for a moment before looking up. "He was way younger."

I pictured the day Special Agent Erickson had come to see me at Chuckie's Chicken. He hadn't had any visible tattoos, and though he'd been intimidating, his gray eyes had been kind. Could *he* have looked at the files? He hadn't asked about Danforth, but was it possible Special Agent Erickson had already made the connection? "Is there anything else you remember about the man? Like eye color? Hair color?"

"No." She batted her eyes at Hemi. "But if *you* give me your phone number, I'll call *you* if I remember something." She slid a paper and pen toward him.

I fought the urge to grab the pen and write my number, and Hemi looked at me with a question in his eyes.

I nodded—because there was no chance Krystal would call if I left my number instead. I wasn't about to leave a lead on the table.

He wrote his number and held out the paper. "Please reach out if you remember anything. It could be important."

She pressed the paper to her heart. "Totally."

After Juanita, Hemi, and I finished reviewing the microfilm and escaped Mousy Voice Krystal, we walked a block to Margo's Boutique where Rochelle worked. The shop's display window contained a mannequin in a forest green power suit with a coordinating handbag.

On a bench outside the store, a skinny guy in sunglasses was reading *USA Today.* When the boutique's bell dinged, he lowered his paper, perked up, and glanced toward the door. But when my brother-in-law exited, the man's face fell, and he resumed reading. His wife must have been taking too long in the boutique.

"Hey, Jason," I said.

"Hey." Surprise registered in Jason's expression as he surveyed us, and he tilted his head as he looked at Juanita. "Juanita, right? I met you at my wedding."

"Yes, nice to see you again," she said. "I hear congratulations are in order."

For a second, he appeared confused. "Oh, you mean the baby. Thanks." His face reddened, and he shoved his hand into his pocket and jangled what sounded like coins or keys.

Juanita stared at him as if she didn't quite know what to think.

"Is something wrong, Jason?" Hemi asked.

"No, no," he said. "I just have a lot on my mind. I'm sorry I can't stick around, but I have some things to do before work this afternoon. Uh, we'll have to get together later. Have a good day." He hunched over and hurried down the sidewalk.

Juanita looked at me and shook her head. When we entered the shop, Rochelle was working alone, steaming new dresses.

Rochelle's eyes widened when she saw Juanita. My older sister was the pretty one in the family—she had our mom's blond hair and bright blue eyes. Her baby bump wasn't showing yet, but she was already stocking up on maternity clothes.

Rochelle set the steam nozzle aside. "What're you doing here?" She hugged Juanita. "What's going on? Did Bobbi Sue do something?"

"Why do you assume I did something?" I examined a navy blazer on the rack next to me.

"Because you dragged Grandma into one of your cases, and that almost got you both killed," Rochelle said.

I bit my lip. "You weren't supposed to know about that." She and Jason had been at his family's cottage at Lake Hideaway during Grandma's and my latest adventure.

"Because of the baby. You and Grandma have been using that as an excuse to keep me in the dark, and I'm tired of it. If something happens to you and Grandma, and Mom and Dad never come home, my only support system is Jason's family."

That was not the reason I'd expected her to give. Hemi was studying my sister. Had her bluntness surprised him too?

"What's so bad about that?" Juanita asked. "They seemed like nice people when I met them at your wedding."

Rochelle swallowed. "They are. I know this sounds ridiculous compared to everything else, but my mother-in-law is an overbearing blabbermouth. If Bobbi Sue, Mom, and Grandma aren't around to fend her off when I go into labor, she'll *insist* on being in the delivery room with Jason and me and then go around telling everyone things I'd rather keep private." Rochelle drew a shuddering breath.

Putting myself in Rochelle's shoes, I realized I had no room to judge. For a second, I imagined being married to Hemi and pregnant. I'd be spazzing out over the possibility of his mother being in the delivery room with me, but I shooed the thought away. Hemi and I were a long way from marriage, and I had a career to think about.

I held up a hand. "I solemnly swear not to die so I can stop your mother-in-law from invading the delivery room and over-sharing with the world."

Rochelle jutted her chin. "I'm holding you to that. And you." She pointed at Hemi. "Had better protect her."

"I plan to."

He was getting a lot of orders from the women in my life, but I took comfort in the fact that my sister was also turning into Grandma Spearman.

There was no fighting genetics.

"Speaking of Jason," Hemi said, "is he okay? We saw him outside, and he acted flustered."

Rochelle went to a shelf and straightened a stack of T-shirts. "He's been acting totally weird lately. He blames work, but even our time at the lake didn't seem to help him relax." She picked up a shirt and refolded it. "I'm afraid he's worried about being a dad and doesn't want to tell me."

"He likes kids," I said. "He's always been willing to help you teach Sunday school."

"I know, but that's different from being responsible for your own kiddos." She turned from the shelf and fixed her gaze on Juanita. "If you're here, there's a reason, so what's going on?"

Juanita and I told Rochelle about the visit from Special Agent Erickson, Dad's secret project to exonerate wrongly convicted prisoners, Morris Fulton being shot dead in Dad's office after renting a townhouse in Wildcat Springs, the keys Dad had given Juanita, and how the Errol Danforth case might be at the center of everything.

"I can't believe you didn't call me last night," Rochelle said. "You're lucky I didn't hear this from someone else."

More Grandma Spearman genetics at work.

"I'm surprised no one told you," Hemi said. "Your grandma had already heard from Judy Beeson."

"Well, *my* friends think Jason and I are at Lake Hideaway. We came home earlier than we'd planned because Jason got called into work yesterday." Rochelle looked back and forth between Juanita and me before she stared at Hemi. "Is there anything else I should know that these two are leaving out?"

"Your grandma is following a lead that we suspect has to do with Danforth, but this morning, she kicked us out of her house and wouldn't tell us what she was planning." He shoved his hands into his pockets.

"That sounds about right." Rochelle rolled her eyes. "I'm trying to wrap my mind around the fact that Mom and Dad leaving town has nothing to do with the drug lord. I can't believe we got that so wrong."

"It was a logical guess," Juanita said.

"Do you think this new information will help us bring Mom and Dad home?" Rochelle snatched the steamer attachment and attacked a rumpled dress. "I want them back before I have the baby in December."

"I do too, but I'm sure Mom wants to be back before school starts in August." I tried to sound confident but didn't quite pull it off since Mom could take a leave of absence.

Juanita removed a file from her messenger bag and held out the newspaper article about Morris Fulton so Rochelle could see his picture. "Have you seen this man around Wildcat Springs or Richardville?"

Rochelle stopped steaming and studied the picture. "No, but . . . when Jason and I came back from the lake, our neighbor Teresa Hawkins told us she was worried about a car she'd seen parked on the street across from our house earlier that day. There was a guy sitting in it and smoking."

I glanced at Hemi. "Did Teresa say the guy was in a car? Not a truck?"

"I think so." Rochelle squinted. "Or I assumed it was a car?

Teresa confronted the man about what he was doing, but he peeled off. She said he had to have been sitting there a while because there were cigarette butts on the street where he'd parked."

"Did she get a license plate or give you a description?" Juanita asked.

"No. She was upset that she didn't get the plate number because she was afraid that he was casing our house while Jason and I were gone." She fiddled with the steamer attachment. "Do you think Morris Fulton was staking out my place because he was hoping to find Dad?"

"Possibly," I said. "But Fulton drove a truck."

Worry clouded Rochelle's eyes. "I don't know. Maybe the situations aren't even related."

"But they could be." Juanita put the newspaper clipping in her bag. "Let's go talk to Teresa and confirm what the guy was driving."

CHAPTER 9

AFTER HEMI, Juanita, and I left the boutique, we drove to Teresa's house. She lived in a bungalow across the street from Rochelle and Jason, and though she was probably in her early fifties, she was in the front yard lounging in a pink kiddie pool with an iced tea in one hand and a Walkman in the other. She wore a purple bikini, and her head bopped to the beat of her music.

"Excuse me, Teresa?" I asked as we approached.

"Hey there!" Teresa removed her headphones as recognition flickered in her eyes. "You're Rochelle's sister—the one who saw the alien."

Juanita glanced at me. "That's not—"

"Oh, I know the story." Teresa waved a hand. "Had to give you quite a turn out there in the woods by yourself."

"You're right." At least that much of the story was true. "Listen, I'm sorry to interrupt your sunbathing, but Rochelle mentioned you saw a man who might've been casing her house while she and Jason were at the lake."

"Sure did. I marched right over to give him a piece of my mind, and he sped off leaving his ciggy butts behind."

"What was he driving?" Hemi asked.

"A minivan—blue." Teresa set her iced tea aside. "I'm just sick I didn't get a plate number."

Probably not Fulton. "Was it an Indiana plate?"

"Yep. I remember seeing the *Back Home Again* slogan—even if I didn't catch the numbers."

"Thanks. That's helpful," I said. "I appreciate you looking after my sister's house."

Teresa beamed. "Happy to help. She was so sweet to water my plants last year when I went on vacay. This was the least I could do."

Juanita held out the newspaper clipping with Fulton's picture. "Is this the man?"

Teresa patted the top of her head. "Hang on. I don't have my readers. Be right back." She hopped out of the pool, and dripping, went into her house—while displaying her buns in a thong bikini.

Hemi's face reddened, and he ducked his head.

Wearing her reading glasses, Teresa reemerged from her house. "Lemme see that clipping." She took it from Juanita and studied it. "Nope."

"Are you sure?" I asked.

"Positive. The man casing your sister's place had smaller features—almost feminine."

Hemi glanced at me. "Do you remember anything else about him?"

"He wasn't a very big guy, and he was wearing a Hawaiian shirt—like Magnum, P.I." Teresa handed the article back to Juanita, then looked at me. "I heard on the radio this morning that Fulton was found dead in your dad's office yesterday evening. Do you think the guy casing Rochelle's place is connected?"

"He could be," Juanita said. "That's what we'd like to help the police figure out."

"Well, I'm rooting for you," Teresa said. "Because if you ask me, there's plenty of shady stuff that goes on around these parts."

"In this neighborhood?" Juanita glanced at a group of boys whizzing past on bicycles.

"In Richard County." Teresa moved her reading glasses to the top of her head and got back into her pool.

"What kinds of shady stuff?" Juanita returned the newspaper clipping to her bag.

"Folks being set up for crimes they didn't commit—like my little brother."

My eyes locked onto Juanita's, and beside me, Hemi inhaled sharply.

"What happened to your brother?" Juanita and I asked in unison.

"He got framed for armed robbery and was convicted." Anger blazed in Teresa's eyes. "Now he's rotting in jail during the best years of his life."

"I'm so sorry," I said. "Is your brother Errol Danforth, by chance?"

"That's right. Glad someone remembers how he got railroaded."

"Actually, Teresa," I said. "We just learned that before my dad left town, he was looking into your brother's case to see if he could help exonerate him."

"Well." She blinked a few times. "That'd be wonderful, but he'd better be careful. Errol wouldn't even tell *me* who he thought set him up—because he feared for my safety. I always figured dirty cops are getting paid to look the other way."

"Like Sheriff Carter?" Hemi looked at me.

"Nah." Teresa scoffed. "He's not looking the other way. He's not looking at all. My best friend used to be married to him, and he's a total slacker who's coasting to retirement."

"Then who do you suspect?" I asked.

"I can't say for sure, but have you *seen* the house Jean Harrell lives in?" Teresa sniffed. "Doesn't seem like someone making a detective's salary could afford a house in the Rolling Hills subdivision, and she doesn't have a husband who makes a good salary to explain it."

I glanced at Hemi. The homes in Rolling Hills *were* pricey, and Detective Harrell had testified in Danforth's case. But Sheriff Carter could be paying more attention than Teresa realized. Had he shown up at the crime scene last night to keep an eye on Detective Harrell since Detective Melchor was on vacation?

We turned to go, but I had another idea and faced Teresa. "Have you visited your brother in the last couple of weeks?"

"No." Teresa sipped her iced tea. "But I'm planning to go see him tomorrow. Why?"

"Could you ask him if he's had a visit or any communication from Morris Fulton?" I asked. "We found evidence that he was helping my dad with your brother's case, and that could be why he was killed."

Understanding dawned in Teresa's expression. "Got it. I can try, but Errol may clam up. I'll let you know if there's anything to tell."

After we left Teresa to her sunbathing, Juanita and I dropped Hemi off at his house because he'd scheduled a phone call with the high school principal who'd hired him. As I drove home, we lapsed into silence, so I cranked up the radio, although there was no way I'd sing along with Michael Jackson while Juanita was in the car. Only God and Eduardo Escort would hear my voice.

"What do you think of your sister's husband?" Juanita asked a few minutes later, when I turned onto the highway.

I'd always thought Jason was average in looks, height, and personality. "He's a nice man who takes good care of my sister."

"Do you think she settled?"

"My opinion doesn't matter as long as she's happy."

"In other words, *yes*."

"Don't put words into my mouth."

"*Is* she happy?"

"I suppose." I kneaded the steering wheel. "She has a lot on her mind with her classes, the baby, Mom and Dad. Jason does too."

"I could tell," she said. "Where does he work?"

"He's a production manager at the automobile assembly plant in Richardville."

"Sounds stressful."

"He just got a promotion, so it is. He wants to be a good provider." I turned off the highway and drove toward Wildcat Woods.

"You don't have to marry the first guy that comes along just to say you're married."

Is that what she thought my sister had done? Since I didn't feel like tugging that thread, I asked, "What if I want to get married because I'm in love?"

"That'd be a great reason to get hitched. *Are* you in love?"

"With Hemi? We just started dating."

"You don't have to be dating to be in love with someone."

I kept my eyes focused ahead as I navigated the winding, tree-lined road. "I care about him." I didn't need to explain myself any further. Why was this Juanita's business?

"He cares about you too."

"I know." I entered my driveway, and when we rounded the bend that led to the house, my heart dropped.

Detective Harrell and Sheriff Carter were getting out of their car.

"Great. I wonder what they want now?" I muttered.

"Let me handle this. By now, they've probably found that letter in the townhouse and just have more questions." Juanita unbuckled her seatbelt and got out of the car with her chin in the air. "Good afternoon. What can we do for you?"

I hopped out and slammed the door.

Detective Harrell approached my car. "Juanita St. James, you're under arrest for the murder of Morris Fulton."

CHAPTER 10

"Call Daniel Wilmington—he's a lawyer I know in Indianapolis," Juanita said to me as I gaped at Detective Harrell and Sheriff Carter. Then, she practiced her right to remain silent as she stared at them defiantly but allowed the sheriff to handcuff her.

I faced Detective Harrell. "You're making a huge mistake. Juanita didn't do this. Did you even call Special Agent Erickson? Maybe he knows why someone wanted to kill Fulton. Why else would the FBI agent ask about him?"

"Ms. Baxter, stay out of this," Detective Harrell snapped but refused to meet my eyes.

Detective Harrell's unwillingness to answer my questions made Teresa's insinuations about law enforcement loom in my mind. Was she setting up Juanita to cover for something illegal she'd done involving Danforth? Is that why she refused to answer about contacting Special Agent Erickson?

"What proof do you have?" I shouted.

"Her prints are all over your dad's office." Detective Harrell set her jaw.

"That doesn't mean she killed Fulton," I said. "You surely need more than fingerprints to arrest her."

"Mind your own business," Sheriff Carter said.

Juanita met my eyes and shook her head as Detective Harrell put her into the back of their car.

"You're in *my* driveway arresting *my* friend, so you made it my business."

"Your parents' driveway." Sheriff Carter sneered at me. "If you keep sticking your nose where it doesn't belong, we'll get you for obstruction of justice."

Even if they had to manufacture evidence?

As his threat hung in the air, fury rose in my chest, sweeping away my fear.

"I'd like to see you try," I muttered as I stalked into the house and went straight to the phone to call directory assistance to get the number for Daniel Wilmington's office. Ten minutes after my initial contact, Daniel's secretary called back to assure me he'd take the case and was on his way to help Juanita.

With this matter handled, I went upstairs, found the notepad with Special Agent Erickson's phone number, and dialed. As the phone rang, I dropped onto my bed, and when he didn't answer, I left a message.

"This is Bobbi Sue Baxter. If you haven't heard, Morris Fulton was shot dead in my dad's construction office. Fulton was helping my dad investigate a man named Errol Danforth, whom they believed was wrongly convicted of a crime. I gave a local detective your card, but she won't tell me if she's contacted you. She arrested Juanita St. James, who's an investigative reporter and family friend, but I don't believe she killed Fulton. I wanted to make sure you knew because the Danforth case may be why my parents fled."

As I hung up, my cat jumped onto the bed with me and perched by my feet. "Things are a mess, Nita."

She licked her paw and appeared unconcerned with my plight.

I dialed Grandma's number and prayed she'd found a lead that would help. As soon as she answered, I said, "What's that you're always telling me about Jean Harrell being a good cop back in the day?"

"She was sharp as a tack. Why?"

"Time is dulling the tack. She and Sheriff Carter just arrested Juanita for Morris Fulton's murder."

"Sheriff Carter? What's that lazy idiot doing sticking his nose in this? Where's Melchor?"

"Vacation." I updated Grandma on what we'd learned after leaving her house. "We already knew Juanita was in Dad's office right before Fulton was killed, so her prints were there, but I don't know what else they've got on her." I twisted the cord around my wrist. "The best way to help her is to find the person who really killed Fulton. Any luck with your lead?"

A few beats of silence passed before Grandma said, "How would you feel about taking a road trip to Michigan with me?"

I blinked. "Are you kidding? We can't leave town. What about Juanita? We're just supposed to leave her here to fend for herself?"

"She has a lawyer and will be out on bond soon enough. In the meantime, if you think you'll get in to visit her, you're not as intelligent as I thought."

I rolled my eyes—even though Grandma was right about visitation. "All right. What's in Michigan?"

"My source, who used to work at the Richardville Paint Factory and no doubt knows Danforth, moved to Michigan to help his daughter run a family camp."

My mind was spinning as I tried to follow this change in direction. "Who's your source?"

"Jesse Joe Darlington."

I'd never heard of him. "You can't *call* Jesse Joe and ask about the factory—and Errol Danforth?"

"When a detective questions suspects, does he call or go see them in person?"

She had a point, but I squeezed the bridge of my nose. "Let me get this straight. You want to drive to Michigan to interrogate a man that you believe could be wrapped up in, *at best*, a frame job and, *at worst*, a murder? What could go wrong?" I let out a hysterical laugh, and Nita stopped grooming herself and appeared as if she resented my interrupting her peace.

"I never said I thought he was guilty—of a frame job or murder," Grandma said. "Besides, I could use a getaway."

"You just got back from a cruise last month."

"I'm restless, and if you're too busy to accompany your widowed grandmother, I'll go by myself."

"You're *not* driving to Michigan by yourself."

"I drove to Florida once when your grandpa was feeling lousy. Besides, I already called Chuckie, and he said it's fine for you to take time off work."

One thing was certain. Grandma was going to Michigan with or without me. But if she believed Jesse Joe had information, a quick trip could be worth our time—and gas—if it helped us figure out who murdered Fulton. "You really believe Jesse Joe can help?"

"We won't know unless we try."

"If we go, we should take Hemi for protection." I braced myself for pushback and prepared to counter by reminding her of his Krav Maga skills.

"Good idea," Grandma said. "It'll give me a chance to get to know him better."

The triumph in her voice gave me the uneasy feeling this had been her plan the entire time. "When do we leave?"

"Pack an overnight bag. Then call the asparagus spear and tell him we're leaving later this afternoon."

CHAPTER 11

"HEMI, you don't have to go the speed limit on my account." Grandma leaned between the front seats of his Bronco. After Hemi had volunteered to drive to Michigan, she'd let me have shotgun because she'd claimed she needed to stretch out in the back. But we were forty-five minutes into the drive, and there'd been very little stretching—and a whole lot of commentary.

"I'm trying to get us there in one piece." He glanced in the rearview mirror as a black Mustang zoomed around us.

"By driving like an old man? At this rate, we won't make it to Michigan before dawn." Grandma tapped my arm. "Crank up the air conditioning and gimme some fruit snacks." She fanned herself with a folded map.

I slipped a packet from the bag at my feet and handed it to her. "Grandma, he doesn't want a speeding ticket." I turned up the air conditioning.

"That's right." He adjusted his sunglasses. "I've never had a ticket."

"You don't say." Grandma ripped open her fruit snacks.

"Do you want to drive?" I glanced at the speedometer. Hemi was going five miles per hour over the speed limit.

"Heavens, no." Grandma leaned back and popped a fruit

snack into her mouth. "I told you, I want to stretch out and enjoy the scenery." She leaned between our seats. "But I'll do that when we get to Michigan. I've seen this part of Indiana a million times, so let's have a little fun first."

"Or we could brainstorm how to help Juanita," I said. "I talked to her lawyer before we left, and he told me she's being held without bond because they think she's a flight risk. I told him to tell her we're chasing a lead."

"What's to discuss?" Grandma shook her head. "You already brought me up to speed on what Rochelle's neighbor Teresa told you, and we don't have any new information, so all we could do is beat a dead horse."

"Fine." I stared out the window at a cornfield.

"What kind of fun do you have in mind?" Hemi asked. "A sing-along? Seeing who can spot the most out-of-state license plates?"

He was such a dork. An adorable one—but definitely a dork.

"I have some questions for you, young man." Grandma popped between us again.

Uh-oh. I could just imagine the headline: "Cross-examination Causes Car Crash."

But Hemi obviously didn't share my concern because he laughed. "Ask away, but could I get some fruit snacks first?"

I couldn't blame him for needing sustenance to endure Grandma's interrogation. I ripped open the package and started to hand them over, but Grandma smacked my arm.

"For heaven's sake, Bobbi Sue, feed him. I don't want to die in a fiery crash because the driver was busy eating."

I shot Grandma a dirty look. "He's capable of driving and eating gummies from a bag." There wasn't much traffic.

She smacked me again. "Such a lack of respect for your elder. I thought your parents raised you better than that."

Hemi winked at me. "You heard her." He opened his mouth like a baby bird.

I fed him a fruit snack, while fighting the urge to pelt him with the rest of the gummies. But *that* would be a distraction, and I didn't feel like dying in a wreck thanks to my overbearing grandmother conspiring with my *friend.*

Did she think my feeding him fruit snacks while she supervised from the backseat was supposed to be romantic?

But he did look cute driving and waiting for the next fruit snack.

Stop it, Bobbi Sue.

I put a grape gummy in his mouth.

"Now, are you ready for my questions?" she asked.

He swallowed. "Fire away." He opened his mouth again, but I widened my eyes. We needed to hear Grandma's question first. I wasn't about to let our driver choke if she asked something outrageous.

Hemi took my hint and clamped his jaw shut.

"How many kids do you want?"

And there it was. Should I hop out at the next stoplight and hitchhike home?

But Hemi didn't flinch. "Two or three. I'd like to have a son and a daughter, but if I have all boys or girls, I'll be content. I'll never make a lot of money, so I have to consider the cost of raising a family."

"Very practical," Grandma said. "How do you feel about being married to a woman with a career?"

My eyes fell on a sign warning against picking up hitchhikers because we were near a prison. *Scratch the hitchhiking idea.*

Hemi didn't answer, and as I was about to reach over and turn on the radio to rid the car of the awkward silence, he said, "I'd need to know that our relationship and our children are top priority, but if they are, I wouldn't mind. My mother worked outside of the home, and she and Dad were happy."

"What names do you like for kids?" Grandma asked.

Oh boy.

Hemi didn't flinch. "I've always liked my own literary-inspired name, so names in a similar style would be fun."

I didn't hate the idea.

"Well, just don't pick anything too weird, or your kids will get bullied."

Hemi chuckled.

"Why'd you break up with your fiancée?" Grandma asked. "I've heard rumors, but I'd like to hear it from the horse's mouth."

I studied Hemi, expecting to see a ticking jaw or white knuckles from gripping the steering wheel, but he didn't flinch and kept just one hand on the steering wheel.

"Leslie and I were together out of habit and moving forward with marriage for the wrong reasons."

"Is my granddaughter your rebound?"

He didn't cringe, which was a marvel.

"Grandma—"

"No, Bobbi Sue. It's cool." He looked at Grandma in the rearview mirror. "Your granddaughter is special to me, and I want to get to know her better because I've had a blast with her this summer."

Warmth spread through my body. "I've had a blast with you too."

He reached for my hand, and I clasped it.

"All right," she said. "That's good enough for me, but get your hands at ten and two, young man. I'd rather not meet my Maker today, even though I'm ready to go if the good Lord sees fit."

"Yes ma'am." He let go of my hand and grabbed the steering wheel.

I held up the bag. "More fruit snacks?"

CHAPTER 12

AT SUPPERTIME, we stopped at Dinty's Diner, which was tucked in amongst a grove of pine trees along a deserted two-lane highway. Hemi parked next to a dusty station wagon, and we filed into the building. Fluorescent lights hummed, and the odors of coffee and grease mingled in the air. On the counter, a revolving display case held peach, apple, and cream pies that looked surprisingly appetizing.

Since a faded sign indicated we should be seated, we picked a booth away from the only other customers—a silent elderly couple sharing a piece of peach pie. A waitress with vacant eyes took our orders for hamburgers and fries and moved back to the kitchen as if she were in a trance.

Grandma leaned forward and hissed, "Is this place giving anyone else the willies?"

"Yes, but I'm hungry, and we haven't passed any other options for miles," I whispered.

"It's the silence." Hemi pointed at a juke box in the corner near a pay phone. "Let's get some background music going." He got up, and as he returned to the table, Elvis started singing "A Little Less Conversation."

"Good choice. I used to sing this to her grandpa." Grandma grooved to the beat and sang along.

I chuckled to myself as I pictured my grandparents in their younger years, and before Hemi sat, he took his wallet from his back pocket, removed a folded paper, and dropped it onto the table.

"I almost forgot about this," he said.

"What is it?" I unfolded the paper.

Grandma stopped singing.

"Right before we left, I figured out why the name Barnaby Feaster sounded familiar," Hemi said. "Mom has me proofread the *Wildcat Wellspring*—or at least she did. Anyway, Barnaby Feaster died last year, and his obituary ran in the paper since he'd grown up in Wildcat Springs."

"No way." I unfolded the paper, which was a photocopy of Feaster's obituary and an article about the single-car accident that'd claimed his life. "Did you have to sneak into the bookstore to get this?" His mother ran the bi-weekly newspaper out of her bookstore office.

"Mom hasn't completely banned me. I can still purchase books at a discount." He gave a rueful grin as he straightened his silverware. "But I went when she wasn't there and searched the back issues."

"Nice work." I nudged him. "You're turning into quite the sleuth."

"Thanks." He winked.

The waitress brought Cokes for Hemi and me and coffee for Grandma before tossing straws on the table and leaving without a word. I handed Grandma the article about Feaster's car accident.

Grandma sipped coffee from the chipped mug as she read. "So he ran off the road and hit a tree. Interesting . . ."

"If he was part of the conspiracy to frame Errol Danforth, was it really an accident?" I skimmed the obituary.

"Exactly." Hemi ripped the paper off a straw. "Then, I thought about the other eyewitness in Danforth's case—Oliver Hoffman."

"Is he dead too?" Grandma asked.

"I don't know." Hemi wadded his straw paper. "I checked the *Wildcat Wellspring* back issues but didn't find an obituary. Obviously, that doesn't mean he's alive and well. It just means I need to do more research."

"But you couldn't because we asked you to go to Michigan." Grandma stood and grabbed her purse. "Lemme make a phone call. I know someone who owes me a favor."

As she walked to the diner's payphone, I focused on Hemi. "This time, I know better than to ask about her source."

"Knowing your grandma, if we ask too many questions, she'll drive off and leave us stuck here." He reached for my hand. "By the way, thanks for letting me tag along."

"We needed a chauffeur." I clasped his hand. "And a bodyguard who knows Krav Maga."

His eyes sparkled. "I feel used."

"But you like the adventure."

He stared out the window as a truck passed on the highway. "Is this what your life will be like when you're an investigative reporter? Spur of the moment trips? Eating in creepy diners?"

"I'm not sure. Why?" I pulled my hand away.

"I just wondered."

I couldn't decide from his tone if he thought that life would be good or bad. Did I even want to know the answer? Was it too soon to ask about his feelings on the matter? If he didn't want to be with me because of my ambitions, it'd be better to know sooner than later.

Right?

Under the table, I curled my fingers into a fist. "And how do you fee—?"

"Well, my old friend Maureen came through. That woman has a memory like an elephant." Grandma returned to our booth and slid in beside me.

Hemi nudged my foot. "Maureen?"

"She's a pal who works in the vital records office back home. I asked if she remembered seeing a death certificate for Oliver Hoffman in the last few years, and she did." Grandma sipped her coffee as if she were enjoying keeping us in suspense.

"And?" I asked.

She set her mug on the table. "Oliver Hoffman died about six months ago—from suicide."

"How convenient for the bad guys." I crossed my arms. "Both eyewitnesses dead."

"That can't be a coincidence," Hemi said.

"I agree," Grandma said. "Because when it comes to crimes and conspiracies, there's no such thing as a coincidence."

Later that evening, the sun was sinking into Lake Michigan as we neared Camp Lakeshore. To our left, water met the purple and orange-streaked sky as Hemi drove the narrow road. On the right were houses nestled among majestic trees keeping watch over the shore below.

"Are we there yet?" Grandma asked in a little-kid whine.

"I take it you guzzled too much coffee back at the diner," I said.

"Yes," she snapped.

I studied the house numbers. According to the directions we'd gotten from a gas station clerk, the camp shouldn't be too much further.

"We made it." Hemi pointed ahead to the right.

"Oh, thank the good Lord," Grandma muttered.

Yes, thank the good Lord indeed.

The painted letters on the faded wooden sign read *Camp hore.*

"Their sign could use some work." The edge of Hemi's mouth twitched as he followed the gravel drive.

I snorted, and a giggling fit took over until I couldn't breathe. Even Grandma chuckled, but as we drove into the woods, our laughter faded when we approached a one-story log cabin—with no signs of life.

"Is this camp even open?" Grandma leaned forward.

"This could be the welcome center that's closed for the night," I said. "Pull up to the door, and we'll see if there's a sign with hours."

Gravel crackled under the tires as Hemi drove closer and stopped by the porch. "I don't see anything."

"I'll check if the door's unlocked." I jumped out of the car before Hemi or Grandma could protest. The porch creaked, so I stepped lightly on the warped boards. I yanked the door handle, but the door was locked.

Moving to the window, I peered inside at a spacious room with a stone fireplace with benches arranged in front of it. A desk was shoved next to another window and was empty except for a rotary phone. To the left was a single door with a restroom sign.

I returned to the Bronco. "It looks like a welcome center, but this camp's been closed for a while. Did you get bad information?"

"I talked to three people, and every last one said Jesse Joe lives here," Grandma said. "Let's keep going and see what else we find."

"All right." Hemi backed up and followed the tree-lined path deeper into the camp.

"This reminds me of Wildcat Woods." I fought a shudder as twilight surrendered to darkness.

The gravel lane came to a T, and Hemi stopped. "Right or left?"

I looked both ways to see if lights shining through the trees would give a clue, but nothing provided a beacon to direct our path.

"Right," Grandma and I said in unison.

Hemi turned, and we continued along, the tires spitting gravel. A buck jumped into our path, and Grandma gasped as Hemi slammed the brakes. The deer stared at us as if we were invading his territory. Hemi honked, and the buck appeared offended as he sauntered forward.

"I see something on the left." I pointed at a light shining through a second-story window.

Hemi drove to the narrow, two-story building with white siding and stopped. A crooked sign next to the door indicated this was the mess hall and the office. An orange cat sitting on the porch railing stood and arched its back.

We got out, and as we climbed the porch steps, the cat leaped from the railing and darted into the woods. Grandma marched to the door and pounded on it. We waited and listened, the wind rustling the trees. Grandma knocked again with more gusto.

No one came, so she jiggled the door handle, and when it turned, she pushed it open. "Anyone home?" She waited a beat before charging inside. "Yoo-hoo! Jesse Joe!"

Hemi clasped my hand, and we followed Grandma into the mess hall. Rustic benches and tables filled the space, and a pass-through window to the kitchen was on the opposite wall. The muffled sound of a TV filtered down the stairs on our right.

"Should we go up?" I asked.

"Not yet." Grandma motioned to a sign for restrooms on the left, so we hurried toward them.

"Let me make sure it's safe, and then I'll guard the door." Hemi brushed past Grandma, flicked on the lights, and poked open the stalls.

"He's a good one," Grandma muttered as she held the door. "You'd better not mess things up with him by caring too much about your career."

"Noted." I suppressed a sigh. Everybody had an opinion on how I should live my life.

Hemi came out. "All clear."

Grandma and I took care of business while Hemi stood guard, and when we were done, he went into the men's room.

"If that's Jesse Joe's TV, he must have it so loud he can't hear the toilets flush," I said.

"Could be." Grandma looked around.

When Hemi came out of the men's room, he asked. "Are we going upstairs?"

"Yep." Grandma charged upstairs, paused on the landing, and shouted, "Jesse Joe? It's Izzy."

What in the world? In my twenty-one years, I'd never, ever heard Grandma refer to herself as *Izzy*. I looked at Hemi, who shrugged.

When we didn't get a response other than a TV laugh track, she continued up the remaining five steps while Hemi and I hesitated on the landing. I was still trying to wrap my head around *Izzy*.

Apparently, Grandma knew Jesse Joe better than she'd let on.

A choking snort caused me to jump, and Grandma snickered as we joined her. I peered around her at a thin, white-haired man with weathered skin clutching a remote and snoring in a worn recliner. He sported denim overalls and a white T-shirt with a hole in the left sleeve. Next to the chair was an end table that held a TV dinner tray with brown gravy remains, a half-empty Sprite bottle, and two hearing aids. A rerun of *The Brady Bunch* blared on TV.

Grandma barreled over to the man and shook his arm. "Jesse Joe Darlington, wake up, and put in your hearing aids! Right this minute!"

CHAPTER 13

JESSE JOE'S arms and legs flew up, and Grandma ducked as the remote sailed past her head. He gasped and clutched his chest. Rubbing his eyes, he glared at Grandma.

"Darn it, Izzy!" he shouted. "You trying to kill me?"

"If you've gotten that soft, I don't know what to say." Grandma put her hands on her hips.

His face broke into a grin, and he put down the recliner's footrest with a pop, stood, and kissed Grandma's cheek. "You haven't aged a bit," he shouted, apparently forgetting Grandma's directive about the hearing aids.

"You're a terrible liar." Grandma snatched his hearing aids and held them out.

"Bossy as ever." But he took the hearing aids.

Hemi and I exchanged glances, and he picked up the remote from the shag carpet and muted the TV. I noted that Jesse Joe was a rather handsome older gentleman.

Jesse Joe inserted his hearing aids. "What in the Sam Hill are you doing here?"

Grandma smoothed her hair. "I need to ask you a few questions."

"Hmph. You could've called. You must've really wanted to see me if you drove all this way." His eyes glimmered.

Did Jesse Joe even realize Hemi and I were in the room?

"Don't flatter yourself." Grandma lifted her chin. "Some conversations are best in person. How else can I know if you're telling me the truth?"

"You callin' me a liar?"

"If the shoe fits . . ."

Jesse Joe scoffed, then flicked his gaze at Hemi and me before looking back at Grandma. "Who've you got with you?"

She hitched a thumb over her shoulder. "That's my granddaughter Bobbi Sue, and the asparagus spear standing next to her is Hemi Miller."

"Howdy." Jesse Joe lifted a hand in our direction but kept his attention on Grandma.

"She couldn't have just called you my *friend*?" I mumbled.

"It's fine," he whispered and rested a hand on the small of my back. "I'm more interested in the show than my nickname. Their chemistry is enthralling."

"Gag me with a *spoon*," I hissed. "You are *so* weird."

"Which is why you like me," he whispered in my ear.

I tried to smother a grin but couldn't, so I elbowed him instead.

"I need to ask a few questions about the Richardville Paint Factory," Grandma said.

"You came all this way to ask me about *that*?" Jesse Joe furrowed his brow. "Why?"

"Long story, but the *Reader's Digest* version is that Guy and Nicki took off unexpectedly in June because my son-in-law got it in his head to fight for people who might've been wrongfully convicted," Grandma said. "He helped free Morris Fulton, who wanted to assist with Guy's exoneration project. They started looking into

Errol Danforth's case. A few days ago, Fulton came to Wildcat Springs and ended up shot dead in Guy's office. Now Juanita St. James, who came to investigate, has been arrested for his murder."

"That's a crazy story, but I don't see how this has anything to do with the Richardville Paint Factory—or me." Jesse Joe fidgeted with his overall strap. "I've been retired for several years."

"But Danforth worked at the factory, and you've heard something about him, haven't you?" Grandma narrowed her eyes. "You only fidget when you're nervous—or upset."

How'd Grandma know that?

"Why don't we sit and chat?" Jesse Joe pointed to the couch across from his recliner.

"That'd be great because I'm confused," I said.

Hemi raised a hand. "Same."

"I reckon you are," Jesse Joe said.

Grandma huffed but joined Hemi and me on the couch while Jesse Joe settled into his recliner.

"First of all, how do you and Grandma know each other?" I blurted because I simultaneously did and did not want to know.

"Years ago, we were engaged until your grandma dumped me."

Now the nickname *Izzy* made a lot more sense.

"You kept flirting with other women," Grandma spat out. "How was I supposed to trust you?"

"She's right." Jesse Joe looked at Hemi and me. "I was immature, but by the time I got my act together, Izzy had moved on with your grandpa. I've never blamed her and reckon things turned out the way they were meant to because my late wife Hazel was a peach. We were married for forty-two years before she passed."

"I'm sorry for your loss," Hemi said.

"Thank you kindly. She's been gone five years, and I miss her every day."

Grandma gave him a sympathetic nod and said, "What've you heard that's got you so fidgety? Did you know Danforth, and why he's claiming he was set up?"

"I knew him. Quiet. A hard worker who did everything I asked," Jesse Joe said. "I was a manager, and believe me, I dealt with all types of folks. Some tried to get by doing as little as possible. Errol Danforth wasn't that kind of guy. You coulda knocked me over with a feather when I heard he was convicted of armed robbery."

"You weren't working at the factory when that happened?" I asked.

"No," Jesse Joe said. "I retired four years ago. Well, if I'm being honest, I was pushed out. The company was sold, and the new owners got rid of old guys like me. They offered us retirement packages and leaned on us until we took them."

"You'd think they would've wanted experienced workers who could help train the younger people," Hemi said.

"In a company where things are being run the right way, that's true," Jesse Joe said. "About a year after I left, I heard from some people who stayed that the new management liked to cut corners."

"How so?" I asked.

"In safety and environmental regulations. When I asked for specifics, nobody would talk."

"I wonder if Danforth witnessed something dicey at the factory," Hemi said.

"You're on the right track." Jesse Joe shifted. "But before I explain why, there's one more thing you should know."

"Spit it out," Grandma said.

"Guy and Nicki showed up on my doorstep about a month ago—and stayed here for a while."

CHAPTER 14

HEMI GRASPED my hand as I processed Jesse Joe's bombshell about my parents. "How long were they here?"

"Are they okay?" Grandma asked.

I leaned forward. "Where are they now?"

Grandma crossed her arms. "When did they leave—and why?"

"I'm confused," Hemi muttered.

Jesse Joe sat up straighter. "Stop with the questions, and I'll tell ya everything I know." He leaned back in his recliner. "Let's start from the beginning."

"Fine." Grandma huffed. "But make it quick."

"After Izzy and I broke up, I moved from Wildcat Springs to Richardville where I met my wife and worked at the paint factory. Hazel and I had three daughters, and our oldest Penny went to college with your mom."

"And Juanita St. James?" Grandma had mentioned her name without further explanation, and Jesse Joe hadn't even questioned who she was.

"That's right. The three of them had an apartment together their senior year." Grandma looked at Jesse Joe. "Go on."

"After college, Penny married Dan, and they bought this

camp and operated it until Dan divorced Penny and left her to manage the place alone. I moved here a few years ago to help after my wife died," Jesse Joe said. "Last summer, Penny decided to close, so I'm holding down the fort until we sell because she moved to Grand Rapids for a new job." He glanced at the TV and fiddled with the remote.

"Mr. Darlington, this background is interesting, but could we *please* get to the part about my parents?" I asked.

"Sure thing, but feel free to call me Jesse Joe. No need for formalities." He drummed his fingers on the recliner's arm. "Your parents showed up early one Monday morning in mid-June. Nicki had a note from Penny, telling me to let Guy and Nicki lay low for as long as they needed—or until the camp sold and we had to clear out. They paid rent for the cabin—cash—and I didn't ask questions. I knew the raw deal Guy got, and I figured he might've seen or heard something in prison that was catching up with him years later."

"They were here and are gone, and you don't know why?" Grandma compressed her lips.

"I never said that, Izzy." Jesse Joe sighed. "I let Guy and Nicki open up on their own instead of giving them the third degree."

Hemi leaned forward. "What'd they tell you?"

"Guy had just learned that Danforth was about to blow the whistle on the paint factory for illegally dumping hazardous materials, and he suspected someone set him up for armed robbery to discredit him."

"Did Dad say where he got the information about the whistleblowing? Because we found a letter from Danforth asking Dad for help, but we don't know if he visited Danforth in prison before he and Mom came here."

"He did," Jesse Joe said. "Danforth told him about the

whistleblowing and how the judge wouldn't even allow his attorneys to use that as part of his defense."

Was the judge part of the corruption too?

"What caused Nicki and Guy to leave Wildcat Springs?" Grandma asked.

"Guy got a threatening phone call telling him that if he didn't stop poking around, he'd end up like Danforth."

"I could see why that spooked him," I said. "Dad's friend Ross had just been murdered, and Dad found his body at a construction site. The detectives were already sniffing around, and he feared they'd pin Ross's murder on him."

Jesse Joe nodded. "That's pretty much what he told me. He thought visiting Danforth in prison tipped off the people behind the setup."

"Did Dad mention Morris Fulton?" I asked.

"He told me he helped Fulton get released from prison—and Fulton wanted to help others," Jesse Joe said. "I got the impression that after the threat, Guy didn't want to involve anyone else in the Danforth case, so he didn't share what he'd uncovered with Fulton. Guy was afraid he had put me in danger by being here, but I told him not to worry. I know how to use a shotgun."

"Where are Guy and Nicki now?" Grandma asked.

"I don't know." Jesse Joe exhaled. "One morning, I woke up, and they were gone. They left a thank-you note under my door but gave me no other information."

I tried to sift through this new evidence. It'd take a while to make sense of everything. "Do you remember the exact date my parents left?"

Jesse Joe stood, shuffled across the living room, and opened the door to the kitchen. He took a calendar from the side of the refrigerator and tapped on a square. "The night of July second. I found their note before I went to church the next morning."

I considered the timing and looked at Grandma. "Mom and

Dad must've passed through Wildcat Springs and dropped the letter into your mail slot themselves because that's the same day you found the letter."

"Sure is," she said.

"If they were trying to lay low, that was risky," Hemi said. "I'm surprised someone didn't see them."

Jesse Joe held up a finger. "That reminds me. While they were here, Guy grew a beard, and Nicki dyed her hair dark brown. Both of them got glasses, and one day, they came back from town with a sack of clothes from the mission. Next thing I know, they're dressing like a couple of old hippies."

"Sounds like they're trying to match the fake IDs I got for them," Grandma said.

Hemi gaped at Grandma, so I drilled him with a stare. "You never heard that."

"Heard what?" Hemi pretended to zip his lips.

Jesse Joe glanced at Grandma with admiration in his gaze. "They bought a VW Beetle and left their truck here. In their note, they promised to come back for it as soon as possible."

Their disguises and new vehicle explained why they risked leaving the letter at Grandma's house. "Where's the truck now?"

"Parked by the cabin where they stayed. It's up the lane from this building a ways. In fact, you're more than welcome to bunk there tonight. It's got two bedrooms."

"Thank you." Grandma yawned. "We'd appreciate that and should call it a night."

He stood. "You folks get your bags out of the car, and I'll be around with the golf cart."

Jesse Joe's golf cart wasn't big enough for all of us, so Hemi and I waited by his Bronco while he drove Grandma to the cabin.

"My head's spinning," I said.

"I know the feeling."

I had so much to process that I needed to think about something else for a while. "On a lighter note, Grandma seems interested in giving Jesse Joe a second chance. Why else would she insist on an in-person visit instead of a phone call?"

"I thought so too." His eyes gleamed. "Do you think she'd ever remarry?"

"Until today, I would've said no, but after watching her spar with Jesse Joe, I'm not sure." I faced him. "Thanks for tagging along. You had to know my grandma wouldn't make the trip easy, so I don't know why you agreed." This wasn't exactly the ideal circumstance for having a define-the-relationship conversation, but I didn't want to wait any longer.

He stepped closer, and his eyes focused on my lips. "Have I not made my intentions clear?"

"I think I could use a little more clarity." I gazed up at him.

"I see." He tipped my chin upward and let his lips hover over mine. "That's not a problem. I intend to make you my girlfriend—as soon as possible."

"Good." I held his gaze as I wrapped my arms around his neck. "Because I intend to let you."

"Now?" he whispered.

"Mmm-hmm."

Our lips met, and he held me closer as the kiss deepened and warmth spread through my body.

"Excuse me, kids."

Hemi and I broke apart and turned toward Jesse Joe who was chuckling in his golf cart. How had we not heard the buzz of the approaching cart?

"I hate to interrupt, but Izzy will wonder where you are if we take too long."

"Yes, she will." I grabbed my bag, scampered to the golf cart, and slid in next to Jesse Joe.

"Sorry about that," I mumbled as I arranged my bag on my lap.

"Don't you worry. I won't tell." He winked. "But she'd have no room to judge even if she did find out. I can think of a time or two we were caught in a lip lock back in the day."

"That's good information to know." I might use it to ward off one of Grandma's inevitable guilt trips.

Hemi stepped onto the back of the cart, and Jesse Joe drove along the path through the woods.

"Jesse Joe, does anyone else besides you and your daughter know my mom and dad stayed here?"

"I can't speak for Penny, but I never breathed a word to anyone. When Penny closed the camp, she let the staff go, so now it's just me."

"No prospective buyers came to look during the time Mr. and Mrs. Baxter were here?" Hemi asked.

"Nope. And Guy and Nicki hardly ever left. I offered for them to go to church with me, but they needed to keep a low profile. Only thing they ever asked me for was a typewriter."

"Did my mom or dad ask?"

"Your mom."

"Did she say why?" The note in Grandma's mail slot had been written in Mom's handwriting.

"No. I told her she was welcome to use the one in the camp office and gave her the key because I didn't need to go in there. I saw them coming out of the office quite a few times." Jesse Joe approached a one-story cabin. Dad's truck was parked next to it.

"I gave your grandma the phone number for the line in my apartment if you folks need anything, but I reckon you'll be comfortable." He reached into his overalls pocket and fished out keys. "These are for your dad's truck—in case you want to check it out in the morning."

I grasped the keys. "Thanks."

"Sleep well." Jesse Joe drove away.

Hemi held the door open for me, and I stepped into a large room with a kitchen in the left front corner, where Grandma was opening and closing cabinets. There was a dining room in the right front corner and a living area on the opposite side. Three doors leading to the bedrooms and a bathroom were arranged along the back wall.

"Bobbi Sue and I are in the room on the right, so put her bag in there." Grandma pointed to the door. "You can take the room on the left."

"Will do." Hemi put our bags away and joined us in the kitchen.

"I thought we could use some tea." She motioned toward the kettle on the gas range and opened a box of tea bags. "There's a chill in the air tonight."

Hemi's kiss had warmed me to the point that I hadn't noticed the temperature, but now that Grandma mentioned it, the cabin was cold.

The kettle whistled, so Grandma removed it from the stove. "Anyone else?"

"Yes, please," Hemi and I said in unison.

Grandma poured the water into mugs, and we took them to the living room and sat on the couch.

"Grandma, do you think Jesse Joe is telling us everything?" I asked.

She fiddled with the tea bag. "We didn't get the whole story about Penny's involvement because he looked at the TV and kept fidgeting when he mentioned her job in Grand Rapids. He was holding something back."

"Of all the things we discussed, it's weird he'd be uncomfortable with that," I said.

"Sure is." Grandma nursed her tea. "I'll have to see what I can get him to tell me tomorrow."

The next morning, I opened my eyes with a gasp, sat up, and blinked in confusion. Sunlight peeked through the checkered curtains, and the twin bed next to me was empty.

Camp Lakeshore.

I fell back against my pillow. I wasn't surprised Grandma was already awake and prepared myself for a lecture on wasting half of the morning in bed. Except . . . I glanced at my watch.

It was 6:03.

Whew. I opened the bedroom door and peeked into the living area. The scent of freshly brewed coffee filtered into the room, and I could see through the window that Grandma was on the front porch with a mug in her hand.

I hurried into the bathroom where I showered and dressed. When I came out, Hemi had joined Grandma outside, and they were chatting.

My heart swelled as I watched their animated conversation. He was special if he was willing to have morning coffee with Grandma. A lot of guys would've stayed locked in their rooms until I finished getting ready.

I found the coffee pot, poured a mug, and joined them outside where birds were chirping. "What's our game plan for today?"

"Good morning to you too." Hemi's eyes danced with amusement.

I sat close to him on the porch swing, and he kissed my cheek, which was fine since Grandma was on chaperone duty.

"Oh, for Pete's sake." Grandma looked back and forth between us. "Are you two *finally* a couple?"

"Yes, ma'am." Hemi said.

"It's about time, so when I go inside, kiss her like you mean it."

"I'd be happy to." He grinned.

"Jesse Joe invited us to breakfast at 7:30," she said. "But after that, I plan to talk to him about Penny, so you and Hemi should take a romantic walk on the beach before we head home."

"Are you planning to use your feminine charms to get Jesse Joe to spill his guts?" I smirked at her.

"I don't know what you're implying, young lady, but Jesse Joe and I were through years ago."

Paybacks were sweet. "But now that you're both single again—"

"I'm not interested in a romantic relationship, so get that idea out of your head. One husband in this life was enough for me."

"But Jesse Joe is a silver fox." I waggled my eyebrows.

"More like a deaf silver fox," she muttered.

Hemi laughed.

"But a silver fox, nonetheless." I winked at Hemi and went inside, but when I passed the living area, the sunlight streaming through the window illuminated the corner of a paper sticking out from under the sofa. I bent and slid it out. The paper was ripped from a small, spiral-bound notebook.

When I recognized Dad's handwriting, my heart rate quickened as I read the words.

Stan Stanton—paint factory chief financial officer. Cousin of Detective Jean Harrell.

CHAPTER 15

"GRANDMA! HEMI!" I shouted. "You've got to see this."

Clutching her coffee mug, Grandma hurried inside with Hemi on her heels. "This better be worth nearly giving me a heart attack. You should know better than to scare an old woman."

My immunity to her guilt trips was strong, so I took her admonition in stride and thrust the notebook paper at her. "Read this. I found it under the couch."

She took the paper, and Hemi peered over her shoulder.

"Stan Stanton knew Fulton was going to Dad's office," I said. "What if Stan guessed Fulton was looking into the Danforth case? He might've followed Fulton, sneaked up on him, and killed him."

"Then why talk to us at Tate's Place and risk implicating himself?" Hemi asked. "All he had to do was sit there, keep drinking his beer, and let us walk away."

"Some people are so arrogant, they can't help themselves," Grandma said. "Does he seem like that type?"

"Yes," Hemi and I said in unison.

"It's possible he paid off Detective Harrell to help frame Errol Danforth." I put my hands on my hips and looked at

Hemi. "Remember Teresa told us Detective Harrell has a bigger house than she should be able to afford on her salary?" I turned to Grandma. "What do you think?"

"I don't know who to trust, and after what happened to your dad, we know anything's possible. If I were to peg one of the detectives as dirty, my choice would be Melchor since he acts like the back end of a horse most of the time."

That was a perfect way to describe him. "Detective Melchor might know people would suspect Detective Harrell because of her family connection to Stan and use that to shift suspicion to her."

"Not a bad thought." Grandma pursed her lips. "But he may not be that smart."

"Plus, he hasn't even been around lately," Hemi said. "So, is it fair to blame him—even if he can be a jerk?"

"Probably not." I wrapped my arms around my waist. Was the entire world corrupt, or were there people out there besides my family and friends who cared about truth and justice?

I wasn't sure anymore.

After a breakfast of Jesse Joe's blueberry pancakes, he'd tossed the office keys to Hemi and me and told us to look around in case my parents had left any clues behind while they'd worked there. I'd checked Dad's truck earlier but hadn't found anything helpful.

The office was down the path from Jesse Joe's apartment, so we followed the sandy dirt trail. The morning dripped with humidity, and I was thankful for the shade from the trees. The office building was a smaller version of the mess hall with white siding, a small porch, and a faded sign. Hemi unlocked the door, and we entered the stuffy building. A reception desk with a typewriter and phone sitting on a phonebook was arranged at the front of the room, and a few chairs with worn orange upholstery sat next to the door.

Hemi motioned toward the phone. "Do you think Jesse Joe would mind if I called home and checked to see if I have answering machine messages? I'm waiting to hear back from the principal about the training I have to do before school starts. I'll leave money for the long-distance call."

"Go for it. I need to get my remote access set up." Instead, I'd have to wait until we were home to see if Special Agent Erickson had called back.

Hemi dialed the phone while I searched the office. I opened the desk drawers and found stray paperclips, pens, and a notepad. Holding up the notepad, I examined it for writing impressions but didn't see any.

When I glanced back at Hemi, he waved me over and tipped the receiver so I could hear.

"I thought of more details about the guy who accessed the Danforth court case records," a mousy voice said.

"Krystal from the courthouse," he whispered, though I certainly didn't need the reminder.

"The guy had buzzed blond hair and was wearing an Aerosmith T-shirt. That's all, but I hope it helps. Buh-bye."

I had to give her a little credit for not trying to steal my boyfriend.

"Does her description help?" Hemi hung up.

Combined with her previous description of a tough-looking guy with tattoos, I could think of only one person with a buzz cut and a penchant for rock band T-shirts. "It sounds a lot like Bruce Reynolds to me."

CHAPTER 16

"WHY WOULD BRUCE BE LOOKING at the Danforth court records?" Hemi sat on the edge of the desk.

"I'm not sure, unless Dad asked him to help, but that would mean he's been in contact with Bruce, and that's definitely not the impression Bruce gave me the other night." I bit my lip. "We should ask Jesse Joe if Mom or Dad ever mentioned Bruce being involved."

"I agree because Juanita's gut feeling about him might be spot on."

"I've always thought he was a nice guy, but now that's what I'm afraid of."

"When we get home, promise me you won't talk to Bruce alone," Hemi said.

"I won't." I looked around the camp office. "Let's keep searching."

Hemi checked a closet, which revealed medical supplies. He scrounged through the closet, inspected the floor, and faced me. "I don't think your parents dropped anything else."

"Nope." I leaned against the desk and noticed a paper sticking out of the phonebook. I opened it to the marked section in the Yellow Pages. Someone had circled the phone number for a local thrift store, but the sticky note marking the page had a different number—and no additional information.

"Jesse Joe said your parents bought secondhand clothes. Maybe they called the mission for directions or hours," Hemi said.

"That makes sense." I studied the handwritten numbers on the sticky note, then pointed at it. "This is my mom's writing, and it isn't a local number. There's a different area code and prefix than the other numbers in this book." I picked up the receiver and punched in the numbers. "Let's see what it is."

I held the phone so Hemi could hear, but an automated voice told us the number had been disconnected.

"Let's check the area-code map." Hemi flipped through the phonebook and found the page that had a United States map with time zones and area-code divisions. "Here. It's a central Florida area code. Do your parents have friends in Florida?" he asked.

"Not that I know of, but they have more secrets than I ever would've imagined, so who knows?" I tucked the sticky note into my pocket. "We should find Grandma so we can head home."

We closed and locked the office door, and Hemi grasped my hand as we strolled the path back to Jesse Joe's apartment. Brush stretched into the wood-chipped trails, and we passed a cabin with a stack of canoes next to it. The entire place felt drained of youthful energy.

Grandma and Jesse Joe met us on the trail coming from the opposite direction.

"Did you find anything?" Jesse Joe asked as we stopped near a fire pit.

"Possibly," I said. "Did Dad ever mention if Bruce Reynolds helped with investigations?"

Jesse Joe cocked his head. "No, but Bruce worked at the paint factory before your dad hired him."

I met Grandma's eyes. "I didn't know that."

"Uh-huh." Jesse Joe nodded. "Remember, I told you about the people who told me there were strange things happening at the factory, but they didn't want to talk?"

"Bruce was one of those guys?" I asked.

"That's right."

"I don't like that coincidence," Grandma said. "How'd you know to ask about Bruce?"

Hemi told them about the message from Krystal at the courthouse. Then, he took money out of his wallet. "For the long-distance call."

"Nah." Jesse Joe waved a hand. "Keep your money. It's my contribution to finding the truth."

"Thank you," Hemi said as we continued back toward the cabins.

"Jesse Joe, do you know Stan Stanton?" I asked.

"Yep." Jesse Joe studied me. "He became the paint factory's CFO right before I retired. He liked to show off his money. Drove a fancy car. Wore expensive suits. He was one of the guys who pressured me to take the buyout. What made you think to ask about him?"

Grandma told him about the paper I'd found on the cabin floor and about Detective Harrell's family connection. "If Danforth was set up, there might be somebody helping on the inside. Stan could've provided the funding."

"Stan gave Fulton directions to Mr. Baxter's office right before Fulton was shot," Hemi said.

"Does sound suspicious," Jesse Joe said.

Just then, gravel crackled, and a car rounded a bend and parked next to the mess hall. A pudgy woman, who looked familiar, emerged from the vehicle and waved at us. She wore a pink floral blouse, khaki shorts, and sandals.

"Well, I'll be. I didn't know Penny was coming." Jesse Joe approached his daughter with open arms, and we followed him.

After they hugged, he said, "You remember Isadora Spearman—and this is her granddaughter Bobbi Sue and her boyfriend Hemi."

"Nice to see you—and meet you." She gave us a warm smile. "Dad called late last night and told me you'd arrived and that Juanita had been arrested for murder. I couldn't sleep a wink, so I got up early and came to see if there was anything I could do to help."

"Penny, do you mind telling us whatever you can about my parents?" I asked. "Any detail that might help us get to the bottom of this situation—and help Juanita."

"Absolutely. It's ridiculous that she's in jail because she wouldn't kill anyone. She doesn't even own a gun." Penny glanced toward the water. "How about we take a walk to the beach and enjoy the view while we chat?"

"That sounds nice," Grandma said. "It might trick me into thinking I'm on vacation—at least for a few minutes."

Even though I was eager to get home, I didn't argue since coming here and not going to the beach seemed like a waste. Jesse Joe took chairs from a storage shed, and we hiked the path out of the camp. After we crossed the road, we took wooden stairs down to the beach.

A few people had gathered with towels and umbrellas, but since there wasn't public access in this area, the shore was quiet. Jesse Joe led us past some driftwood where we arranged our chairs in a semicircle. Haze hovered over the lake, mingling the sky and water into a single, mysterious entity.

"All right." Penny adjusted her sunglasses and told us about my parents showing up on her doorstep without warning and how she'd offered to let them stay at the camp.

"Did anyone else know my parents were here besides you and your dad?" I asked.

"I didn't tell a soul." She held up her hand as if on the witness stand.

"Your dad said that my parents requested a typewriter and that they used the one in the camp office," I said. "Do you know what that was about?"

She stared out at the water and bit her lip. "Well . . . maybe. But I don't think it has anything to do with why they're hiding."

"If you know something, spit it out," Grandma said. "This situation is escalating, and we need to get to the bottom of it because we can't count on the cops when they've arrested an innocent woman."

Penny glanced at her dad. "Did you mention my new job?"

"Nope." Jesse Joe shook his head.

She folded her hands in her lap. "I'm a literary agent, and I told your dad that if he got bored while hiding out, he should write a book about his experience of being set up, charged, tried, and wrongly convicted for a crime. I could sell a story like that. At first, he told me he didn't have the talent, but your mom said she could help. I gave them information on how to write a non-fiction book proposal and gave your mom some direction on how to frame the story and write the sample chapters. If they were using the typewriter, I'd bet it was for a book, but I don't know for sure."

I considered Penny's words as the waves of Lake Michigan lapped against the sand. A few kids splashed in the water while their parents watched from the shore. "Is there anything else you can think of that might help us get a handle on what's happening?"

Penny sat in silence for a moment. "The morning they left

my house, I overheard a conversation while I was making them breakfast. Your dad mentioned calling someone named Rick," Penny said. "Does that name mean anything to you?"

"No," I said.

"It does to me." Grandma faced me. "He's your dad's second cousin who lives in central Florida."

CHAPTER 17

I THOUGHT of the Florida phone number in my pocket. "Why do you think Dad thought Rick could help?"

"He's a private eye," Grandma said. "Unlike some of your dad's other family, Rick never believed your dad was guilty and did what he could to help, even though it was Juanita who eventually cracked the case."

I racked my brain as I tried to remember Rick, but I couldn't. After we'd moved to Wildcat Springs, we hadn't seen my dad's family much. I took the sticky note with the phone number out of my pocket. "We found this Florida number in the office phonebook." I handed it to Penny. "Do you recognize it?"

She examined it. "No, but it looks like your mom's writing." She showed it to Jesse Joe. "You didn't write this, did you, Dad?"

"Nope."

"We called, but the number's been disconnected," Hemi said. "Do you know where Rick lives in Florida?"

"Last I heard, he lived in a town called Honeybell, but that could've changed," Grandma said.

"I wonder if Mom and Dad went there to get Rick's help."

Grandma stared out at the lake. "Could be."

"And if so, why?" I stood and folded my chair. "We need to head home and figure out what's happening with Juanita. I don't want her to feel abandoned."

"I can't believe she was arrested for murder—and is being held without bond." Penny scowled as she picked up her chair. "Clearly, the detectives in Richard County are incompetent."

After everything that'd happened this summer, I couldn't disagree.

That afternoon we returned to Wildcat Springs. Hemi dropped Grandma off at her house, and as we drove away, I said, "I want to talk to Bruce Reynolds."

"I figured. Should we try your dad's office?"

"Sounds good."

He drove to the office and warehouse, but when we arrived, crime scene tape fluttered on the front and back doors. However, there was a sign on the front door, so I got out to look. Eileen had written that the office was closed until further notice but had left her name and home phone number for clients to call.

I got back into Hemi's Bronco. "Bruce was working at the Keller house the other day. Let's check there on the way out of town."

Ned Keller and his wife Doris lived on the highway outside of Wildcat Springs, and they attended my church. They'd hired Dad's company to add on a living room, half bathroom, and a deck. When we arrived, a truck sat in the driveway, and since I knew the Kellers, I led Hemi around to the back of their house, following the sound of a buzzing saw and the thwacks of hammers.

In the back yard, I caught a whiff of freshly cut lumber, and three men were framing the addition. I didn't recognize any of them. "I'm Bobbi Sue Baxter, and I'm looking for Bruce Reynolds," I said. "Do any of you know where he is?"

Two of the men hammering stopped and gawked at us.

After a few seconds of awkward silence, the third man at the table saw said, "You Guy's kid?"

"Yes."

He adjusted his tool belt and faced me. "Well, you deserve the truth. Bruce and his family took a last-minute vacation. He stopped by yesterday morning in the family van with his wife and kids. Said they were headed out. Even had one of those big cargo carriers strapped to the roof."

Interesting timing for an impromptu trip. "Where'd they go?"

"He didn't tell me." The man shrugged. "Just that his family needed a break. Like I said, it was a last-minute deal."

"Do you know when they'll be back?" Hemi asked.

"Dunno." He shook his head. "I guess it doesn't matter as long as we get paid. I called Eileen right away, and she had no clue about Bruce leaving but assured me that all is well in the money department, and that we could expect our payment."

"Thanks for your help—and for being dependable," I said.

"No problem. If you want my advice, you might want to step in and make sure your dad doesn't lose his business. Without Bruce around, projects won't get done like they should. Not everyone is as dependable as my team." He resumed sawing a board.

Hemi and I walked around the Keller's house in silence, and when we were out of earshot, I said, "I don't like this at all."

When I got home, I dumped my bag on the kitchen floor and made a beeline for the blinking answering machine. Nita emerged and slinked around my legs as I pressed *Play*.

"Bobbi Sue, it's Misty. I'm dying to know what happened on your picnic with Hemi. Call me."

The machine beeped.

"It's Misty. Did you get my first message? I need details about your date. And don't even try to tell me you don't know about that poor guy who was murdered in your dad's office. Call me."

Another beep—and a message from a couple hours ago.

"This is like the third time I've called." Misty's voice had elevated an octave from her previous messages. "Where are you? I stopped by your house on the way to work, and you weren't home. And you weren't at Chuckie's either. What's going on? Why are you keeping me out of the loop? Are you trying to solve the murder of the guy killed in your dad's office? You know I'm helpful! Call and at least tell me you're alive! I'm working at the inn this afternoon and evening."

The machine beeped again. "Bobbi Sue, this is Teresa—Rochelle's neighbor. I visited my brother this morning and have some news. I don't wanna talk on the phone, but I'm meeting a friend at Tate's Place at 5:30. I've seen you there before, so if you get this message and wanna stop by, we can talk."

The answering machine quit, and I sighed. Even though I was disappointed I hadn't heard from Special Agent Erickson, Teresa's message intrigued me.

Glancing at my watch, I decided I had time to make a quick trip to Creekside Inn so Misty and I could chat before I met Teresa. After taking a moment to freshen up, I grabbed my keys and headed out.

The inn was near a little burg called Venlap, which was a short drive from my house through Wildcat Woods. My dad's construction company had renovated the historic brick mansion, and since the grand opening, the inn was drawing tourists from around the country who wanted a getaway in a peaceful, wooded setting.

I parked in the gated lot, got out, and nodded to a few guests milling around the front porch. When I entered, Misty was working behind the oak reception desk. She wore a burgundy polo with the inn's logo, which I felt confident was an assault on the reigning Soybean Queen's fashion sense.

As soon as she saw me, she tossed her red hair over her shoulder and put her hands on her hips. "Where have you been? I've been freaking out!"

I blew out a breath. "A lot's happened in the last couple of days."

She glared at me. "Tell me about it."

I looked around the lobby, and we were alone. "What exactly do you know?" I whispered as I leaned against the desk.

Misty dropped her hands to her side and picked up a copy of the *Richard County Gazette* lying on the counter. "Morris Fulton was shot dead in your dad's construction office, and your journalistic idol Juanita St. James was arrested for his murder and is being held without bond." She smacked the newspaper and tossed it onto the counter. "What gives, Bobbi Sue?"

"My dad helped clear Fulton's name after he was wrongfully convicted, and Grandma, Hemi, and I believe Fulton was killed because he came to town to help someone else who may've been wrongly convicted."

"Oh wow." She gaped at me. "We're going to need a snack." She set a bell on the counter, emerged from behind the desk, and headed toward the breakfast room. "How does Juanita figure in?"

We were alone in the room, and I followed her through the maze of tables to a sideboard with an assorted cookie tray, water pitcher, and coffee carafe. "I called her to ask about Morris Fulton, and she took time off from work to come help us."

She nabbed a snickerdoodle, took a bite, and motioned for me to help myself. "I'm so lost right now. Why'd you do that?"

Of course she was lost. I hadn't told her about Special Agent Erickson's visit. So, as I filled a coffee cup, I shared how we now believed my dad's investigative activities were the cause of his leaving town with Mom, and the drug lord we'd believed to be a threat—wasn't. "That's why I called Juanita, and she came to visit the day Fulton was killed. She even had keys to my dad's office and safe that he'd sent her years ago, and she went there to see if Dad had left information that could help."

"Was there anything?" She polished off her cookie.

"No. But that put her at the murder scene—and it doesn't look good that she visited Fulton's hometown and asked questions. They think she followed him here."

"Anything else I should know?"

There were so many other things I could say, but I chose the tidbit I knew would interest her most. "The picnic didn't go as expected, but . . . Hemi and I are officially a couple."

She squealed and clasped her hands. "I *knew* it. You're perfect for each other. I'm *so* happy for you!" Then, her smile faded. "What'd his mom say?"

I gulped lukewarm coffee and tried to put Amanda out of my mind. "She doesn't know yet . . . or maybe she does, and Hemi was afraid to tell me."

"What I wouldn't give to see the look on her face when she finds out." Misty snatched a chocolate chip cookie and broke it in half. "I'm guessing you were out on a date last night when I stopped by. I need details."

"I wasn't on a date. Hemi, Grandma, and I took a road trip to chase a lead in Michigan."

"A road trip. With your grandma." She gaped at me. "Ohmygoodness! Are you *trying* to sabotage your relationship with Hemi?"

That hadn't been the reaction I'd anticipated, but I could roll with it. "If he's the right guy, Grandma won't scare him away. She already asked what he wants to name his children."

She groaned. "How'd he take it?"

"Didn't faze him. He gets a kick out of her."

"If you say so." She finished the chocolate chip cookie, brushed crumbs from her hands, and pulled out a chair at one of the tables. "Back to the case. Tell me more about this lead in Michigan."

I joined her at the table. "Grandma's former fiancé Jesse Joe Darlington used to work at the paint factory in Richardville but now lives in Michigan, and we wanted to see what he knew about a former employee—Errol Danforth. Dad and Fulton were investigating Danforth's armed robbery conviction because they believed someone framed Danforth to stop him from blowing the whistle on environmental violations at the factory."

"Whoa. Back up one sec." Misty blinked at me. "When was your grandma engaged to Jesse Joe?"

"Before she met my grandpa."

"This gets better and better." She folded her arms across her chest as realization dawned in her expression. "Hold on. Tim worked the Danforth case—with Jean Harrell. Didn't they find Danforth's gun in a dumpster?"

"That's right." Her memory was impressive.

"And weren't there two eyewitnesses at the convenience store who swore under oath that Danforth was the robber?"

"Yes, but one of them died in a single car accident last year and the other of suicide six months ago."

"That's fishy." She bit her lip. "If both eyewitnesses are dead, your dad suspected a frame job, and Fulton was investigating

Danforth's case and was murdered. . . Wait a sec. You guys suspect law enforcement involvement, don't you?"

My stomach tightened. "It would make sense, wouldn't it?"

Color drained from Misty's face. "Tim and my mom have been on vacation in California and got back this morning, so even if he knew about Danforth being set up, he didn't kill Fulton."

"Your stepdad can be a jerk, but I don't see him killing or framing anyone." As much as I didn't like Detective Tim Melchor, I really believed that, and Misty probably needed to hear me say it.

"I don't either." Misty hopped up, took a butter cookie, and returned to our table. "Is Jean working the Fulton murder case?"

"Yes. And Sheriff Carter made an appearance at the crime scene with Detective Harrell to arrest Juanita. It feels a little weird because I've not seen him around this summer. It's almost like he was keeping an eye on Detective Harrell."

"I can't believe Jean would help frame someone." She shoved the entire butter cookie in her mouth.

"I don't want to believe it either, Misty, but where'd she get the money to buy her fancy house?"

Misty swallowed. "Her uncle, who didn't have kids, left her a big inheritance a couple of years ago. She hasn't always had money. For years, she lived in a crappy apartment." She put her elbows on the table and rested her head on her hands. "Is there any evidence that points to Jean besides her house?"

"Her cousin Stan Stanton is the CFO of the Richardville Paint Factory, where Errol Danforth worked, so it's a connection. Stan gave Fulton directions to my dad's office and could've followed him to kill him if he suspected Fulton was onto their scheme."

"Stan Stanton," Misty murmured. "That chubby guy who

comes into Tate's Place almost every day after work? Big gold watch?"

"He's the one."

"You really think Jean was involved?"

"I don't know, Misty, but someone in law enforcement being in on this makes sense."

"I know." She leaned back. "If you're right about the corruption, then what if Juanita wasn't released on bond because the judge is in on the cover-up?"

"That would make sense." Was it the same judge who hadn't allowed Danforth's defense attorney to present the whistle-blowing information?

"We probably should stay out of this, but I can tell from the look on your face that you won't," Misty said. "What's the next move?"

I told her about my plan to meet Teresa at Tate's Place. "I might catch Stan Stanton there too."

She glanced at the grandfather clock in the lobby. "My shift ends in about fifteen minutes. Can I come with?"

"Absolutely," I said. "And I can be your wingwoman while you flirt with Kurt."

CHAPTER 18

MISTY and I arrived at Tate's Place as patrons were filtering in after work for happy hour. "Need You Tonight" by INXS blared on the juke box in the corner of the dimly lit room. Kurt was working behind the bar and wore an Indianapolis Colts T-shirt. His face lit up as soon as Misty entered. I followed her to her usual perch at the bar but didn't see Stan Stanton—or Teresa. ESPN was playing on the TV mounted above the bar, but no one seemed to be watching.

Before I could say hello, Misty blurted, "Big news, Kurt! Bobbi Sue and Hemi are officially a couple!" She squealed.

Normally, such a declaration wouldn't bother me, but there were two problems. First, Misty's voice got louder in her excitement—as usual. And second, just as she let the world know, Hemi's mother Amanda sailed around the corner from the restrooms and froze upon overhearing Misty's broadcast.

Misty got her wish to see the look on Amanda's face, and the mixture of a grimace coupled with disbelief didn't disappoint. I could imagine the headline: "Local Bookstore Owner Drops Dead Over Son's Choice of Girlfriend."

Without a word, Amanda unfroze and pursed her red lips. With her floral skirt swishing elegantly, she stalked to the booth where her boyfriend Willis Brooks was waiting. I'd often thought that if *Absentmindedness* were a fashion magazine, he could be the cover model because of his perpetually disheveled appearance. However, since he started dating Amanda, he wore ironed shirts, although tonight one shirt sleeve was rolled up while the other was buttoned, and he'd still forgotten to shave.

I had no idea how Misty and I had overlooked her Uncle Willis when we'd entered, but I blamed my focus on the investigation and her feelings for Kurt.

While Misty clasped her hand against her mouth, Kurt chuckled and filled her beer mug. I slid off my stool, squared my shoulders, and approached Amanda and Willis's table.

"Would you give us a minute, Bobbi Sue?" Willis issued a charming smile while a hint of sympathy glimmered in his eyes.

"No, no. That won't be necessary." Amanda directed her gaze at me. "How long have you and my son been a couple?"

"Since yesterday." Adding more detail would be a horrible idea. Knowing I'd taken a road trip with him—even with a chaperone—would finish her off.

Some tension vanished from her rigid posture and expression. "I see." She pointed to the seat next to Willis. "Sit."

He scooted over to make room, and I obeyed.

"I would've preferred to hear this news from my son, but considering you just became a couple yesterday, I'll give Hemingway the benefit of the doubt and assume he planned to tell me when he had the chance."

Hemi hadn't even told his mother he was moving, so remaining silent seemed like a good choice.

"It'll take time for me to get past my disappointment that my son and Leslie ended their engagement," she continued. "I'm not thrilled that he's jumping into another relationship so quickly, but if you're comfortable being his rebound, then who am I to stand in your way?"

Willis shifted as if her cattiness made him uncomfortable, but his face remained expressionless.

Run while you can, Buddy.

Indignation rose in my chest, but I literally bit my tongue. How could I argue? The same thought about being his rebound had crossed my mind. Were Hemi and I doomed? Spewing an argument would give her ammunition for the future if things went wrong, and I couldn't let her get into my head because that was what she wanted.

So I said, "I'm glad we have your blessing."

"I wouldn't go that far," she snapped.

"Anything else you'd like to discuss?"

She made a shooing motion with her fingers. "Run along. I'm confident you have an investigation to stick your nose into since you found a dead man in your father's office." Her tone clearly indicated that this was yet another black mark against my dad—and my entire family.

I scooted out of the booth. "When I solve the case, I'll give you the scoop for the *Wildcat Wellspring*."

She narrowed her eyes. "I prefer to consult reliable sources."

Wasn't being this nasty exhausting? "Enjoy your evening." I tossed a fake smile at them, held my head high, and rejoined Misty at the bar.

"Ohmygoodness, I'm *so* sorry." She rested her hand on my arm. "I'm *such* a blabbermouth bimbette."

"True," I said. "But Amanda would've found out eventually, and—" My gaze landed on Stan who was plopping down at the opposite end of the bar. "Stan just walked in."

"Are you *positive* you aren't mad at me?" Misty asked.

"Not at all. No matter when Amanda heard, she wasn't going to be happy about Hemi and me dating. You kept us from delaying the inevitable." I got up and went to the stool next to Stan.

"Hey there, Alien Girl. I heard you found Fulton." He fidgeted with his watch.

Alien Girl? "We did."

"It's a shame. I feel awful about giving him directions to your dad's office. If I'd have known what he was walking into, I would've never butted in."

"You had no way of knowing he was in trouble." The bags under his eyes had become trenches. Guilt? "Or did you?"

He glanced around. "I don't know what you think you know, but I was sitting right here at this bar around the time Fulton was killed in your dad's office. After I gave him directions at the gas station, I came straight here." He pointed at Kurt. "That bartender is my alibi." He waved Kurt over.

Interesting how Stan had provided an alibi without me asking. It's not like I was a cop.

Kurt approached and leaned against the counter. "What can I get for you, Stan?"

"My usual—and tell Alien Girl I was here Wednesday afternoon sitting on this stool and watching the end of *The Geraldo Rivera Show,* waiting to meet my cousin. I couldn't have killed Morris Fulton." He pointed at the screen above the bar.

"He was." Kurt set a bowl of peanuts on the counter. "I changed the channel for him, and he met Detective Harrell." He slid the mug to Stan. "He's not your guy, Bobbi Snoop."

As Kurt walked away, Stan gave me an I-told-you-so look and took a swig of beer.

Stan's need to establish an alibi bothered me because it indicated he had a hunch about what'd happened to Fulton—and fear was keeping him silent. "Do you know Errol Danforth?"

"Name sounds familiar." Stan clutched his beer mug with both hands. "Why?"

"He worked at Richardville Paint Factory until he went to

prison for armed robbery. Since you're the CFO, I thought you might know him."

"I don't know everybody."

That wasn't exactly a denial of knowing Danforth. "How long have you worked there?"

"Long enough."

"Did you know Jesse Joe Darlington?" I asked.

"Yep." Stan fiddled with his watch. "When the new owners made us get rid of the good guys like Jesse Joe, the place went downhill fast."

"How so?"

"Can't say."

"Can't or won't?"

Color drained from his face, and he glanced around. "Look, I've got less than two weeks until I retire, so I'm trying to stay under the radar."

"If you know something, speak up," I whispered. "A man died, and I'm confident that someone tied to the paint factory is involved."

"I didn't kill him."

"But I think you suspect who did."

"Then you're thinking wrong." He stood. "But I'll throw you a bone because you seem like a nice kid trying to find the truth." He glanced at Misty, and his gaze stuck like putty until he ripped it away. "That beauty queen friend of yours isn't the only person watching your six, right?" He tipped his head toward Misty.

"I have a boyfriend."

"Good." Stan looked around and leaned in. "You're on the right track asking questions about the factory—and Danforth."

"How so?"

He took another look around. "A couple of days ago, I was interviewing a candidate for my replacement, and about halfway through, it became as plain as day he had no intention of taking the job and was just sniffing around trying to get an inside look."

That was interesting. "What'd he ask?"

"He had questions about accounting practices and wanted to know if we'd had an external audit recently." Stan drummed his fingers on the bar. "We did last year, and I told him so. At first, I thought I was interviewing a conscientious guy—until he asked if there was any truth to the rumor that workers had been paid to keep quiet about safety violations a few years ago."

"Is there?"

"I dunno. That's the first I'd heard of it, and if workers were paid hush money, it didn't come through the company books, or I'd have known." He held up both hands. "I swear on my dog Bandit's life."

That was a dramatic statement, but my gut told me Stan was being truthful about the hush money. Anyone covering up a crime would know better than to leave a financial trail. "What about Danforth? Why am I on the right track there?"

"Because Mr. Nosy specifically asked if Danforth took hush money, but again—I didn't know."

"By the way, what *was* Mr. Nosy's name?" I asked.

"Greg Jenkins. He was a shrimpy guy with brown hair and big glasses. Looked like the type who got stuffed in a locker back in high school, and now he's out to make the world pay for it."

"Anything else you remember about him?"

"Yeah," Stan said. "I couldn't figure out why he'd want to move to Indiana from Florida."

CHAPTER 19

THE NOSY JOB candidate from Florida couldn't be a coincidence. "Do you remember what city Greg Jenkins was from?"

Stan squinted. "No, but he mentioned he wasn't too far from Orlando."

Central Florida. I'd have to ask Grandma if she knew what Rick looked like, but if he was a "shrimpy guy," then maybe Dad had hired Rick to investigate, and he'd posed as Greg Jenkins and taken the interview to get answers.

"Have you told Detective Harrell about your suspicions about what's happening at the paint factory?"

"No. She doesn't like to talk about work, and I respect that."

What a convenient excuse. "Do you think local law enforcement could be involved in a cover-up?"

"Dunno. I trust Jean, but if the hush money rumor has any truth, the people running the show would need help, right?" He shifted. "Not sure I trust Sheriff Carter, but I don't trust any elected official—from either party." He unearthed his wallet from his back pocket.

"Anything else?" I asked.

He tossed a bill onto the counter. "In my estimation, the

safest thing for you to do is butt out and watch your six." He waddled away as he stuffed his wallet into his pocket.

I checked my watch, and since it was 5:45, I glanced around for Teresa. She was sitting at a table with Jane White from Willow Haven. When Teresa saw me, she waved me over, and I joined them.

"Bobbi Sue, this is my best friend Jane," Teresa said. "We've known each other since high school."

"Nice to see you again, Jane." I slid out a chair and sat.

Jane studied me as if she couldn't quite place me. "Were you the one asking questions about my new tenant the other night when I was out walking Velda?"

"That's right."

"Shame what happened to him. The cops came and searched his apartment. I don't know if they found anything helpful or not." Jane nursed her martini. "Teresa was just filling me in on how Morris Fulton's death might be connected to what happened to her little brother a few years ago."

"Potentially." I turned to Teresa. "What'd Errol say this morning when you visited?"

"As usual, he didn't want to say much about the case, but I got him to confirm that Morris Fulton visited him on Tuesday afternoon."

"Did Errol tell you anything else?" I asked.

"He warned Fulton against investigating the case. When I told him your dad had investigated it and been threatened, he said he wasn't surprised and told me to drop it." Teresa looked at Jane. "Are you sure you can't convince Ralph to reopen Errol's case? There's got to be something we can do."

Jane compressed her lips. "Sweetie, he didn't listen to me when we were married, so he's certainly not going to listen to me now." She turned to me. "Back when the sheriff's department was eyeing Errol for that crime, I *begged* my ex to look at other suspects. I used to babysit Errol, and he was such a sweet kid. There's no way he robbed that store." She popped her olive in her mouth. "This girl right here is more likely to find the truth than that toothpick-gnawing idiot I wasted twenty-six years on."

I was glad I wasn't drinking, or I would've spewed liquid. I pressed a fist to my mouth, and when I regained my composure, I asked, "You're talking about Sheriff Carter, right?"

"Yep. He's too busy planning retirement and chasing skirts to care about a wrongful conviction." Jane shifted her gaze across the bar, and her eyes followed Amanda and Willis, who were leaving. "Speaking of that, I heard he even tried his luck with Her Majesty Amanda Miller and struck out." She snorted. "I wish I could've been there to see the look on his face."

Teresa flinched, folded her hands, and looked at me. "I'm sorry I don't have more to help you, but my brother is scared." She slid her glass of wine over to Jane. "I don't feel like finishing this."

"I appreciate your trying." I stood, thankful Teresa was giving me a cue to leave. "Enjoy your evening."

"Wait, Bobbi Sue," Jane said.

"Yes?" I turned back.

"When we got here, I noticed you were talking to Stan Stanton. He wasn't hitting on you, was he?" She polished off Teresa's wine.

"No, why?"

She set the glass on the table. "I've known him for years, and he thinks he's God's gift to women." She rolled her eyes. "I was just going to offer to run interference if he ever bothers you again."

"I appreciate the offer, but I know how to handle myself."

Jane chuckled. "I believe you."

I ordered a tenderloin and ate it at the bar while bringing Misty up to speed. An hour later, I decided it was time to get home to see if Special Agent Erickson had left me a message. I dropped a tip on the counter. "I'm heading out."

Misty tore her focus from Kurt. "Keep me posted—and let me know if there's anything I can do to help."

"Will do." As I walked toward the exit, a towering man with piercing eyes stepped into my path. He wore a gray suit that appeared expensive and carried a leather briefcase.

"Bobbi Sue Baxter?"

Who wants to know? But I fought the urge to voice the thought and said, "Yes."

"Daniel Wilmington." He handed me a business card. "We need to talk about Juanita St. James."

I glanced at the card. "Here?"

He looked around and then pointed. "That booth. Away from people." He plowed past me and claimed a corner table as if he were conquering uncharted territory.

I slid in across from him. "Do you want to order?"

"No. I can't stay long, and this won't take much time." He glanced around. "Why is that redhead staring?"

I followed his gaze. "That's my friend Misty. She's wondering who you are." When I shook my head at her, she stuck her lip out and rotated toward the bar.

"I'll cut to the chase," Daniel said. "Juanita stumbled into a hornet's nest here in Wildcat Springs. Her life's been threatened, so she's being transferred to a facility with better security. She wanted me to tell you to stay out of this mess—don't even put in a request to visit her."

"If I don't investigate, who'll find the truth to clear her

name? Who'll find justice for Morris Fulton—or Errol Danforth? She taught me the truth always matters."

"She told me you'd use her words against her."

"But—"

"I have a team of investigators. We'll handle Juanita's defense, and part of that is figuring out who killed Fulton, because she didn't. She wants you and your sister to be safe." He set his briefcase on the table, opened it, and produced an envelope. "For you. Juanita said you might not believe me since I'm a stranger."

I took the envelope—that wasn't sealed—and removed the letter penned in Juanita's handwriting.

Dear Bobbi Sue,

This case has become more dangerous than I ever could've imagined. If you wanted a taste of the risks involved in being an investigative reporter, this can be your baptism by fire. That said, don't worry about me. My lawyer's team will take care of the investigation as they build my defense.

Prioritize finishing college, looking after your sister, and dating Hemi. I know you want to take down bad guys, but your fight doesn't have to look like mine. There are many ways to battle evil. Maybe your way is to be an investigative reporter. Maybe it's not. Whatever you decide, stay strong, be safe, and remember the truth always matters, but it doesn't always have to be your job to uncover it.

Sincerely,

Juanita

I stared at the words as they became blurred through my tears. Did she not think I was capable? I tucked the note into my purse and refocused on Daniel. "What evidence have you found to help her?"

"I can't talk about that." His tone made it clear the matter wasn't debatable.

I wasn't shocked. "Will you let me tell you what *I've* learned? In case it could help your team?"

"Absolutely." He took a legal pad and pen from his briefcase. "Go."

I shared our Richardville Paint Factory corruption cover-up theory and how Errol Danforth might've been ready to blow the whistle. I shared my suspicions about local law enforcement being involved and how Fulton had visited Danforth in prison the day before he'd died. Finally, I told him I'd attempted to contact Special Agent Erickson.

Daniel finished scribbling notes and returned the pad and pen to his briefcase. "This is where your investigation should end, Miss Baxter, but if you hear anything else, please call me. We're dealing with dangerous people who'll go to great lengths to cover their tracks." He snapped his briefcase shut. "I'll be in touch if Juanita wants me to pass along any more messages." He strode out, and because Misty was engrossed in conversation with a friend who'd joined her at the bar, I slipped out before she could give me the third degree.

As I drove home, I found it impossible to turn off the questions running through my head. Could I trust Daniel Wilmington? Was this case as dangerous as he wanted me to believe? I kneaded the steering wheel as I entered Wildcat Woods and followed the winding road through the trees.

Telling me to quit didn't seem like something Juanita would do, but unless someone had forged her handwriting, the letter was authentic.

I arrived at home, and as I got out of my car, an eerie feeling swept through my body—followed by a chill. But there was no reason to feel cold on a muggy July evening. Shaking off the sensation, I walked around the car toward the house. When a stick caught my sandal, I tripped.

As I stumbled forward and regained my balance, a rush of air whizzed past my head—and my car's windshield shattered.

CHAPTER 20

A BULLET. From the woods behind the house.

The danger registered, and I darted across the driveway to take cover in front of the house. Had a trespassing hunter made an errant shot?

A second bullet grazed my arm, leaving a stinging red trail—and sweeping away doubts that a sniper was hunting me.

A third shot pinged against the gutter as I rounded the corner, bolted toward the front door, and prayed there wasn't a second sniper waiting on this side of the house.

Fumbling with my keys, I found the one for the house. With shaking fingers, I took at least three tries to insert the key into the lock. I threw open the door, slipped inside, and locked it. Staying away from the windows in the back of the house, I flew to my dad's office.

My heart thudding, I slammed the door and pushed the couch in front of it. I left the lights off, and yanking the curtain closed, I dove for the floor safe, opened it, and removed a gun. With my arm throbbing, I lunged for the phone and dialed 911.

"A sniper in the woods behind my house shot at me three times. A bullet grazed my arm, but I got away and am locked in the house. I'm afraid the shooter's going to break in." I gave my address.

"Ma'am, stay on the line, and keep pressure on your arm."

I looked around but didn't see many good options for soaking up blood and chose a throw pillow. I put the phone between my head and shoulder and pressed the pillow against my arm.

"Ma'am, are you still with me?"

"Yes. I barricaded myself in the house with a gun."

"Are you bleeding a lot?"

"The bullet just grazed my arm, so it's not gushing. How long will it take for help to get here?"

"Deputies are on their way."

That wasn't an answer. Living remotely had its disadvantages. I listened for breaking glass or more shots, but I only heard my breaths coming in short gasps. I checked if my gun was loaded.

It was.

My pulse thrummed against my neck as I squeezed my eyes shut. If my sandal hadn't caught on that stick, my head would've looked like my windshield, and I would've been hanging out with Grandpa Spearman in heaven.

"Are you there?" the dispatcher asked.

"Yes," I said. "I don't hear anyone entering the house—yet."

Seconds ticked by, and I strained to listen. Would I hear broken glass, the whiz of another bullet, or the wail of sirens? If someone had ordered a sniper to take me out, would Rochelle, her unborn child, and husband be in danger too?

What about Grandma?

Mom and Dad—wherever they were?

And Hemi.

I closed my eyes as the thought of losing loved ones made me woozy.

Or was I getting weak from blood loss? I opened my eyes and checked the blood-stained pillow. No. There wasn't much blood, and the bleeding was slowing.

I drew my knees to my chest. How much longer? Surely, the sniper would realize I'd call the police and would take the opportunity to escape. Right?

But whoever wanted me dead would try again.

"Ma'am?" the dispatcher said.

"I'm here."

"There was a sheriff's deputy not too far from your house, and he radioed that he'll be there any minute. Stay inside."

No kidding.

Just then, I heard the siren, so I hung up and called Hemi.

As soon as he answered, I blurted, "A sniper tried to kill me."

"Where are you?"

"Locked in Dad's office at home."

"Do you have your gun?"

"Absolutely." I heard more sirens. "I called the cops, and they're here. Will you—?"

"I'll pick up your grandma and be right there."

The deputies had arrived and had found no trace of the sniper, and since the bleeding on my arm had slowed, I refused to go to the hospital but let Jack, the EMT, come into the kitchen and clean and bandage my wound while I sat at the table.

Grandma and Hemi joined me, and Hemi kept getting up and looking out the sliding door at the woods. As Jack finished and wished me well, Detective Tim Melchor came inside.

I'd never been glad to see him before, but tonight I was relieved the man that Hemi and I had dubbed Detective Girly

Hands was back from vacation with a sunburned bald head as a souvenir.

"We found shell casings near the tree where we think the sniper was hiding," Detective Melchor scooted out a chair and dropped into it. "It wasn't that far from your car, so you're lucky you tripped because any decent shooter wouldn't have missed such a clear shot."

I gulped. "God protected me."

He grunted. "Any idea who's got it out for you?"

"It'd be hard to say." How could I answer that? I didn't trust him enough to say I suspected corruption in the sheriff's department.

He narrowed his eyes. "You sure?"

"Did the sniper leave behind any other evidence?" I asked.

"No," Detective Melchor said. "You've been poking around in Fulton's case, haven't you?"

"It doesn't matter whether I have or haven't," I spat out. "I don't deserve to be picked off in my yard!"

Grandma put a hand on Detective Melchor's arm. "Your questions can wait until tomorrow."

"Fine." Concern flickered in his eyes, replacing the annoyance. "But you shouldn't stay here alone—or even at all. Why don't you give Misty a call, and the two of you can stay with my wife and me until we catch the shooter?"

This was the nicest thing Detective Melchor had ever offered.

"That won't be necessary," Hemi and Grandma said in unison.

"She'll stay with me," Grandma said.

"And I'll be there to watch over both of them," Hemi added.

Detective Melchor looked back and forth between them. "You could be a target too, Isadora."

"I know how to use a gun, and so does Bobbi Sue." Grandma

hitched her thumb at Hemi. "And he knows Krav Maga." A note of pride tinged her voice.

Was this Grandma's way of saying she approved of Hemi? And why was I worried about that at a moment like this?

Detective Melchor stood and pushed in his chair. "I'll send a deputy to check on your house."

"I won't protest," Grandma said. "Thank you."

Shaking his head, Detective Melchor went outside.

"Grandma, we won't be safe at your house either. What if someone at the sheriff's department is in on this scheme, and the person they send finishes the job instead of protecting us?" I asked. "Maybe Jason's family wouldn't mind if we stayed at their cottage on Lake Hideaway."

"My uncle has a cabin there too," Hemi said. "I'd be happy to ask him if we could use it."

"You're both right, but I have a better plan." Grandma glanced around, then met my eyes. "Before Hemi picked me up, I called Jesse Joe. He's on his way in his plane, and when he lands at the Richardville Airport, we'll be there to meet him. You, your sister, Jason, and I are getting the heck out of Dodge." She faced Hemi. "We've got room for one more. You in?"

"Absolutely." There wasn't the slightest hesitation in his voice.

I gazed at him, and he clasped my hand. "Where are we going?" I asked.

She leaned forward. "Honeybell, Florida."

CHAPTER 21

"ARE we going to find Dad's cousin Rick?" I asked.

"That's what I was thinking." She looked between Hemi and me. "He's the best lead we've got right now, and maybe we can get him to tell us if your parents reached out for help."

"I agree." I told them what I'd learned about Greg Jenkins from Stan Stanton earlier that evening. "Grandma, would you say Rick is a 'shrimpy guy' who got stuffed in a locker during high school? Because that's how Stan described the guy that he interviewed."

Grandma chuckled. "That sounds about right. He's like a little dog with a big bark *and* bite, so I'd say anyone who tried to stuff him in a locker paid a hefty price." She stood. "Now go get packed."

Later that night, Grandma, Hemi, Rochelle, Jason, and I sat in a row of orange vinyl chairs with bags at our feet in the deserted terminal of the Richardville Municipal Airport. We were waiting for Jesse Joe to arrive, watching through the floor-to-ceiling windows for the plane's lights to pierce the darkness. We glanced around as if we expected someone to charge into the terminal and take us out.

The silence grew heavier and heavier until Jason popped out of his seat and announced, "I need a snack. Anyone else?"

Grandma, Rochelle, and I shook our heads. The thought of eating junk food made my stomach churn.

Hemi rose and walked toward the vending machines with Jason.

Rochelle rested her hand on her belly. "Grandma, can we trust this Jesse Joe person? What if he's in on the cover-up? He worked at the paint factory."

"Your parents trusted him enough to stay at the camp with him," Grandma said. "He's a good man."

I didn't share Grandma's full confidence in Jesse Joe, but Mom and Dad relying on him went a long way in building my trust, and at the moment, he was our best option.

"Jesse Joe left the paint factory before the questionable things started happening—and the bad guys wanted him out of the way because he has integrity," I added.

Rochelle fiddled with her blouse's hem. "Why do you keep putting yourself in danger, Bobbi Sue? It's awful even when it's just you that the bad guys are after. Now all of us are dragged into the mess."

"This isn't my fault," I snapped. "I didn't ask to find a dead body in Dad's office or get shot. And I had nothing to do with that guy casing your house."

"Wait." Rochelle's eyes widened. "Do you think the sniper was also the person casing our house?"

That was a good question. "I don't know, but whatever is happening goes way beyond anything I ever did—or didn't do."

"But you always have to find answers, and people know you don't rest until you do." Rochelle's eyes flashed.

"I didn't start this." I squeezed my hand into a fist. "Dad did with his investigation hobby!"

"Girls, that's enough!" Grandma snapped. "We'll never figure this out if you turn on each other. Rochelle, you can bury your head in the sand, but evil still exists. We have to stop it when we have the chance because it can swoop in and get you even if you're keeping your head down pretending it's not there. Bobbi Sue, be smart, and don't take unnecessary risks. Have I made myself clear?"

"Yes," I muttered.

Tears welled in Rochelle's eyes. "Got it."

"Good." Grandma crossed her arms.

"Speaking of avoiding risks . . ." I swallowed over the lump in my throat. "Juanita gave her lawyer a letter to share with me. She asked me to stop investigating because it's too dangerous." I took the letter from my purse and handed it to Grandma.

She held it so Rochelle could see, and when Grandma finished reading, she said, "She might change her mind if she knew you'd almost been picked off at your own home. You're in this whether you want to be or not."

Grandma always had such a heart-warming way of getting to the point.

She gave me the letter, and we lapsed back into silence until Jason and Hemi returned with candy bars.

"I've been thinking. Why Florida?" Jason unwrapped a Snickers. "We could hide out anywhere and wouldn't have to go so far away."

"I was wondering the same thing," Rochelle said.

I glanced around to ensure we were alone in the terminal before I told them about Dad's cousin Rick from Honeybell.

But before I could share, Grandma blurted, "The further away, the better. Jesse Joe's old buddy Marion runs a fancy resort, and we can stay there for cheap since it's the offseason.

Who knows how long we might have to lay low, so we might as well do it in luxury." Something in her tone and expression warned me not to say another word.

"How long are we staying?" Jason chomped his candy bar.

"Until it's safe at home," Grandma said with a note of annoyance in her voice.

Rochelle squeezed her eyes shut and leaned her head on Jason's shoulder. Hemi put his arm around me and drew me closer as a pinprick of light appeared in the darkened sky.

After Jesse Joe took a break and refueled his Piper Cherokee Six, we stowed our bags, boarded, and donned our headsets. Grandma sat in the cockpit with Jesse Joe, Jason and Rochelle sat in the middle row, and Hemi and I took the back. Our goal was to get to Tennessee, where we'd stay the night before continuing to Florida.

As the plane taxied the runway and took off, Rochelle squeezed Jason's hand. Hemi put his arm around me, and I leaned in. There was so much I wanted to say. Had his mother told him about our showdown at Tate's Place? Would her reaction matter to him?

He took off his headset, moved mine aside, and edged closer. "You look like you have something you need to get off your chest."

I took off my headset and scooted closer so we could hear each other. "Your mom knows about us. Misty blurted it out at Tate's Place, and your mom and Willis overheard."

"I know." Amusement danced in his expression. "They paid me a visit earlier this evening."

I grimaced. "I'm sorry."

"I'm not. She'll get used to the idea when she sees how happy you make me." His gaze traveled to my lips.

If we hadn't been crammed on a small plane with my grandma, Jesse Joe, my sister, and brother-in-law, I would've kissed him. Instead, I fought to focus my thoughts. "She's going to hate me forever when she finds out her only child ran off to Florida with his girlfriend who was almost taken out by a sniper."

"She'll get over it if she wants me in her life." He laced his fingers through mine. "There's nothing I want more than to figure this out with you. You're worth the risk."

"Are you sure?" But I didn't really need to ask.

The intensity of his gaze spoke for itself.

"Yes. I love you. I know it's awkward timing to tell you now," he whispered. "But I don't want something to happen without me telling you how I—"

I kissed him, and when I broke away, I whispered, "I love you too."

He gave me another quick kiss and donned his headset.

I put mine back on too, in time to hear Grandma say, "You two behave back there, or I'm going to split you up."

My face burned, but we all laughed—which we desperately needed.

CHAPTER 22

A FEW HOURS LATER, in the middle of the night, we landed at a small airport in Tennessee where Jesse Joe had stopped before. He'd picked this airport for our refueling stop because there was a motor lodge across the road. After he secured his plane in a hangar, we gathered our luggage and walked across the quiet highway to the motel. The limestone building had about ten rooms in a U shape on either side of the lobby, and a pink neon sign flickered, advertising vacancy.

As we approached the lobby entrance, Grandma removed her wallet from her purse. "I have cash to cover the rooms." We crowded into the wood-paneled space that smelled of stale cigarette smoke.

The greasy young man working behind the front desk stifled a yawn. "Welcome."

"Do you have three rooms available?" Grandma asked.

"Sure do." He took her cash and handed over the keys.

"Hemi, you can bunk with Jesse Joe in room twelve." Grandma passed Jesse Joe a key as we stepped outside. "Bobbi Sue with me in three, and Rochelle and Jason in nineteen." She gave Rochelle a key, then turned to Jesse Joe as we went back outside into the fresh air. "What time are we leaving in the morning, Captain?"

"Let's shoot for ten," Jesse Joe said.

"Sounds good. Sleep tight, and don't let the bedbugs bite." Grandma snapped around and marched toward our room.

I cringed. *This joint better not have bedbugs.*

I muttered to Hemi, "Meet me at the ice machine in five." I nodded toward the vending machines behind the breezeblock wall.

While Hemi, Jesse Joe, Rochelle, and Jason went the opposite direction, I followed Grandma to our room and dumped my duffel bag on the bed's faded floral comforter. After she went into the bathroom, I found the ice bucket, slipped outside, and headed for the machine.

Hemi rounded the corner, and he held up his ice bucket with a grin. "Good call."

I took Hemi's bucket and set it with mine on top of the ice machine. "We didn't get to say a proper goodnight." I wrapped my arms around him.

He bent, and our lips met—until a nervous chortle interrupted.

We jumped apart.

Jason stood next to the machine with a bucket in hand. "I came to get ice, but it looks like I need to ice you two down." He looked pleased with himself for making the corny joke. "Your secret's safe with me." Jason's awkward chuckle mingled with the growling ice machine, and when he finished, he saluted as he ambled away.

Hemi and I burst into laughter.

"What are the odds he tells your sister?" Hemi asked.

"There's no way he's keeping that from her, but honestly, I don't care. I can think of a time or two I caught them kissing."

"Speaking of Jason and Rochelle, why do you think your

grandma wasn't forthcoming with them about why we're headed to Florida?" He wrapped his arms around me.

"I'd guess she's worried about Jason not keeping his mouth shut. According to Rochelle, her mother-in-law is quite the talker."

"Fair enough."

I rested my head on his chest. "I want this to be over."

"You'll—*we'll*—figure it out."

Even though I had Hemi by my side, the longer this saga continued, the more I wanted a normal life.

He kissed me again, and I floated back to my room. But halfway there, I stopped. *The ice bucket.* I returned to the machine where both of our buckets were sitting on top. After I filled them, I walked toward Hemi and Jesse Joe's room.

As I rounded the corner, I heard Jason shout, "I never asked to be dragged into this. I have a wife and unborn baby to think about." He stood at a payphone with his back to me.

Who was he talking to? And more importantly—what'd he revealed? I stepped around the corner to eavesdrop.

Jason listened, then snapped, "I gave you an idea. It's not my fault it didn't work."

What idea? That was a weird statement if he was telling someone back home about our situation. Not to mention, I'd never heard my affable brother-in-law use that tone with anyone.

Ever.

Jason paused. "Well, I'm the least of your worries. We're squared up, and I told you—I'm out." Jason hung up, clenched his fists, and bowed his head. He lingered at the phone as if he were trying to gather his composure.

Squared up? I stepped from behind the wall. "What's going on?"

Jason whipped around, and his eyes widened. "Bobbi Sue! What're you doing out here?"

"Hemi and I forgot these." I held up the ice buckets. "Are you all right? You sounded upset."

"Uh-huh. I, uh, had to call my boss and let him know I'm going to, uh, be out for a while. He wasn't happy about it. There's a lot going on right now, but he, uh, has the reports he needs." He shifted back and forth.

No one who wanted to keep a job called his boss at two in the morning. Something else was going on, but I decided to play dumb. "You called in the middle of the night?"

"He, uh, works second shift like me, and it, uh, takes him a while to unwind after he gets off work. He doesn't go to bed until around three."

"Wouldn't the phone wake his family?"

"What are you? Colombo?" Jason scowled. "He's a bachelor."

"I see." I turned to go, but since he'd called me Colombo, and I was feeling like a smart aleck, I stopped. "Just one more thing."

"Yeah?" His face remained blank, and not a hint of understanding flashed in his eyes.

Okay, then. "You didn't tell your boss where we're going, did you?"

"No." He huffed and puffed. "I told him I'm out for a while. I'm not a complete moron."

So . . . he was calling himself a partial moron? "Goodnight, Jason."

He shoved his hands into his pockets and stomped away. Shaking my head, I found room twelve and knocked.

Hemi answered, and when he saw the ice buckets, he said, "I guess we were a little distracted."

"Just a little." I handed him a bucket and glanced over my shoulder. "I just witnessed something weird."

After he set the ice inside, he stepped out and closed the door. In a whisper, I told him about the phone call I'd overheard and Jason's defensiveness.

"His reaction is weird unless he was embarrassed because you caught him being rude to his boss."

I bit my lip. "But something doesn't feel right."

"I believe you. We'll see how he acts tomorrow," Hemi said. "We're in a stressful situation, so maybe that's all it is. If not, then time will tell." He wrapped his arms around me. "Come here so I can steal another kiss."

I was more than happy to oblige.

CHAPTER 23

THE NEXT AFTERNOON, Jesse Joe landed his plane at Honeybell Regional Airport. Our journey from Tennessee had been uneventful, and Hemi and I had both finished novels and then swapped. Jason had been his affable self and had relaxed enough to fall asleep and serenade us with his snores.

I'd never been to Florida in the middle of summer, and as soon as we stepped off the plane, I understood why. Humidity soaked my face, and my back immediately began to sweat. Heat shimmers rose from the runway.

"Whew, boy." Grandma fanned herself. "It's hotter than Satan's armpit out here."

Jesse Joe chuckled and shaded his eyes. "Sure is. Let's get inside and see if Marion is here yet."

We hurried to the stucco terminal, and when the sliding glass door swooshed open, chilled air greeted us. A few retirees milled around, and a single vending machine stocked with Tab and RC Cola hummed in the corner.

"There she is." Jesse Joe waved and beamed at an attractive woman with short gray hair. "Marion! Over here!"

Grandma muttered, "*She?*"

As Marion approached, I guessed she was in her late sixties, but she wore a black tank top that displayed arms with a definite lack of waddle and shorts that showed off tan and toned legs.

Beside me, Grandma bristled, and Rochelle looked at me with raised eyebrows. Jason put on a baseball cap and ducked his head as if he were fighting a laugh, and I couldn't blame him. When Grandma had described Jesse Joe's "old buddy," I'd pictured a guy.

Apparently, I wasn't the only one who'd made that mistake.

"Welcome to Honeybell!" Marion displayed her perfect teeth.

She bear-hugged Jesse Joe—long enough to make Grandma clear her throat so loudly that Judy Beeson probably heard all the way back in Indiana. When Marion stepped away, she surveyed us as Jesse Joe made quick introductions.

"I'm so glad you're here. I'd do *anything* to help Jesse Joe—and his friends." She rested a hand on his shoulder and batted her eyes at him.

I bet you would.

Hemi coughed, but this time, Jason didn't bother to disguise his chuckle. I had so many questions, and I glanced at Rochelle, who shot me a warning look as if she knew I was about to flip my interrogation switch.

"Let's get to the resort," Jesse Joe said. "I can't wait to see what you've done with the place."

"Right this way." Marion led us outside to the parking lot. "I could've sent one of my employees to pick you up, but I wanted to welcome you myself."

"We surely appreciate that, Marion," Jesse Joe said.

Grandma looked away, but not fast enough for me to miss her eye roll.

"How do you and Jesse Joe know each other?" I blurted as the heat blasted my face again.

Marion stopped beside a white van with *Goldenvale Resort*

emblazoned on the doors. "My late husband Bill was the pastor at the church Jesse Joe and his wife Hazel attended in Richardville, and Hazel was one of my *dearest* friends. We kept in touch even after Bill was called to serve at a church in Ohio."

I caught Jason's eye as we climbed into the van, and he appeared a little spooked. Frankly, I didn't blame him because I wasn't thrilled that someone with connections to Richardville knew our whereabouts. How many more friends did Marion keep in touch with?

"Jesse Joe told you we don't want people knowing we're here, right?" Grandma asked. "Especially folks from Indiana."

"Of course, Isadora," Marion drawled. "I always respect my guests' privacy."

"How'd you end up running a resort in Florida?" Hemi asked.

"I'm a Florida native and moved back here to be closer to my daughter and son-in-law after my husband died." Marion got into the driver's seat and started the engine. "I'd always dreamed of running a resort, and this has been a perfect second act."

"What was your first act?" Hemi asked.

"I was a stay-at-home mom."

Jesse Joe sat in front with Marion, and as she left the airport parking lot and drove onto a highway, she peppered him with questions about his daughters and life at Camp Lakeshore. The road took us past orange groves and strawberry fields. At a crossroad, a sign pointed toward Honeybell, but Marion followed the road that looped around a lake. In the distance, buildings were clustered along the lakefront.

"Is that Honeybell over there?" Hemi asked.

"Yes," Marion said.

When we arrived at Goldenvale Resort, Marion drove past an iron gate and traveled a lane lined with palm trees. We passed a sprawling Spanish-style building where a towheaded boy in floaties led his young dad toward the pool, and a yuppie couple in tennis attire strolled past a burbling fountain.

"That's the lobby, recreation, and convention space, and you can check out our restaurant, The Golden Spoon, when you get a chance. Our chef makes the best seafood dishes in Honeybell," Marion said. "I'll take you right to your villa so you can get settled, but later, if you're feeling adventurous, follow the path around Lake Sereno, and you'll end up in historic Honeybell."

"It's a little hot for a walk," Grandma muttered.

"I've provided some golf carts," Marion said. "Feel free to take them downtown. Lots of people do."

"That's mighty kind of you, Marion," Jesse Joe said.

She waved a hand. "Here we are."

Our villa was Spanish style, like the main building, with cream-colored stucco and red roof tiles. Two golf carts were parked in the driveway, and each cart had room for four people.

After Marion drove away, we filed inside. The kitchenette, living room, and dining room stretched to our left with views of the lake outside their windows, and the three bedrooms were arranged around a courtyard with lounge chairs and pink hibiscus plants.

After Grandma assigned rooms, Jesse Joe announced he was going to the pool, and Rochelle and Jason said they wanted to go too. I collapsed onto the couch in front of the TV and made up an excuse about needing a nap because I hoped Grandma, Hemi, and I would search for Rick. Hemi took the hint, joined me, and channel-surfed through the myriad cable channels. When Rochelle, Jason, and Jesse Joe left, I found Grandma unpacking in our room.

"Want to talk about it?" I opened my duffel bag sitting on my twin bed.

"It would've been nice if Jesse Joe had mentioned his friend Marion is a woman."

"Why should it matter?"

Grandma unzipped her suitcase, yanked out a skirt, and shook it out. "Because she's a hussy."

"That hussy is providing a nice place for us to stay at a steep discount."

"Exactly. No one is that generous." Grandma wagged a finger at me. "You mark my words. She has her eye on Jesse Joe."

"I told you. He's a silver fox." I dropped onto the bed. "Does this mean you like him?"

"I never said anything of the sort," Grandma huffed. "I just don't want to see him get sucked into that woman's wiles."

"Wiles? She was a pastor's wife," I said. "She's probably a nice person."

"That's what those women want you to believe, acting sweet and pious, but I've met a few pastors' wives in my day that couldn't be trusted. I can spot a hussy a mile away, and I know that Marion woman is up to no good."

"Like we're all in danger . . . or just Jesse Joe?" I'd learned a long time ago not to discount Grandma's intuition.

She seized a blouse. "Any widower within a thousand-mile radius of Marion is in danger. As for the rest of us, well, I hope we didn't make a huge mistake staying here since she used to live in Richardville."

"Me too. I'd like to think she meant what she said about respecting privacy." I ran my hand over the comforter. "Could we talk about the plan to find Rick?"

"Absolutely." She zipped her suitcase and stowed it in the closet. "Let's go."

We found Hemi in the living room still channel surfing.

"We have work to do, so shut off that TV," Grandma said.

"Yes, ma'am." Hemi obeyed.

Grandma held up a paper. "I found an address for Rick's office in your mom's book."

"It's Saturday, so I doubt he's in," I said. "Did Mom have his home address too?"

"Nope. And I couldn't find it in the phonebook either," she said. "Let's go to the office and see what we find, but if Rochelle, Jason, or Jesse Joe asks, all we did was buy groceries. I don't want to worry your sister any more than we already have. Got it?"

"Got it," Hemi and I said in unison.

If Rochelle asked too many questions, I wasn't sure I'd have the answers.

Before Grandma, Hemi, and I left Goldenvale Resort, we took the golf cart to the lobby, found the concierge, and picked up a map of Honeybell. According to the address, Rick's office was located downtown on Main Street. Since we didn't have another vehicle, and no one wanted to walk in the heat, Hemi drove the golf cart around Lake Sereno while Grandma chided him for driving like an old man. I tuned her out and stared at the glimmering water and the people paddle boating.

Marion's mention of historic Honeybell had caused me to picture a vibrant district with many shops and restaurants. But when we reached the town, I was surprised to see several colorful buildings arranged around a town square that appeared dilapidated and abandoned.

A donut shop and a shoe store had closed for the day. A faded orange awning publicized Honeybell Market, and a sign indicated it was open until eight. Tía Rosa's Cocina was also open, and a hint of cumin spiced the air.

I double-checked the map and address. "We're on Main Street, but I don't see Rick's office. It should be right here."

"Look at that window." Hemi pointed to the building next to the restaurant where residue from removed window stickers remained. "Rick McCann, Private Investigator." He parked the golf cart behind a red station wagon.

"Great," I muttered.

"That explains why the number you found at the camp was disconnected," Grandma said.

"If it was even Rick's number." I glanced at a gray sedan parking beside the curb. Signs advertising Tía Rosa's Cocina were on the car's doors. A young man wearing a baseball cap with the Mexican restaurant's logo got out and headed for the alley between the restaurant and Rick's former office.

"Excuse me, sir?" I waved as he turned. "Could you please help us?"

"Sure." He stopped, and we approached him. His red polo had the name *Mateo* stitched on the front in white.

"Do you know Rick McCann, P.I.?" I motioned toward Rick's old office.

Mateo surveyed us with his dark eyes. "He's a customer—or was."

"Do you know why he closed this office?" Hemi asked.

"Not sure." Mateo adjusted his baseball cap. "Last week, when I came to work, his sign was gone. I asked my tía Rosa about it—she owns the restaurant—and she thought his lease was up." A hint of uncertainty flickered in Mateo's eyes.

"But you don't agree?" I asked.

"Well, whenever Rick ate here, I'd asked if he had any exciting cases, and most of the time, his job sounded lame. He was always trying to find proof that somebody's husband or wife was cheating." Mateo adjusted his hat. "But a few days before he closed his office, he mentioned he was going undercover in another state. He didn't give me details, but maybe it's one of those deep cover ops like you see on TV, and that's why he closed his office."

"Or he moved to a new location," Grandma said. "Is there anyone else who might know where he went? A secretary? Friends? It's important for us to talk to him."

"Rick was a one-man show and always came to the restaurant by himself." Mateo glanced toward Rick's old office. "I shouldn't tell you this because Tía Rosa wouldn't be happy, but one time, I delivered food to Rick at home. He lives on North Grove Street and rents a garage apartment. I can't remember the house number, but the main house has gnarly pink flamingos stuck everywhere. Unless you're blind, you can't miss them." Mateo looked toward the restaurant. "I gotta get to work. Later."

"Thanks for your help," I shouted as he walked toward the employee entrance. Then, I turned to Grandma and Hemi. "Time to go find some gnarly pink flamingos."

Using the town map, I navigated while Hemi drove to North Grove Street. The modest neighborhood had bungalows and ranch-style houses, and soon we came to a property with pink flamingos lining the driveway like guards. Next to the house was a detached two-story garage.

"This has to be the right place." Grandma poked her head between us. "Who in their right mind decorates with that many flamingos?"

Hemi parked the golf cart, and we climbed the rickety stairs to the apartment entrance where I knocked on the paint-chipped door. When no one answered, I knocked again and said, "Rick? It's Bobbi Sue Baxter—Guy's daughter. I'm with my grandma and boyfriend. If you're here, we need to talk." I tried opening the door, but it was locked. "I guess we go back to Goldenvale and try again later."

"Check under the doormat." Grandma pointed at the mat with a faded flamingo.

I stepped off the mat, and Hemi bent and lifted it, revealing a key.

He held it up. "We're not going to use this, are we?"

Grandma snatched it from his hand. "You bet we are. We have no idea how long it'll be until Rick gets home, and we didn't come all this way not to find answers." She unlocked the door, and it creaked open.

We stepped into the studio apartment with a full-size bed, a worn couch, and a kitchenette. Through an open door was a small bathroom, but it was the green chalkboard hanging on the paneled wall above a desk that caught my attention.

A web of notes was scrawled in yellow chalk, and my heart tumbled when I focused on the name in the web's center circle.

Jason McKeever.

CHAPTER 24

I STUDIED the notes surrounding Jason's name on Rick's chalkboard. *Richardville Paint Factory employee from 1983-1985. Took hush money to ignore environmental regulation violations. Involved in Danforth setup?*

I'd always thought my brother-in-law was a dweeb, but he was good to my sister, and she loved him. Plus, it wasn't like *I* had to be married to him.

But a criminal? Is *that* why I'd heard him get so angry on the phone last night? Why he'd acted weird and defensive?

Finally, I said, "This must be a mistake. Jason's completely devoted to Rochelle."

"Two things can be true," Hemi said quietly.

I needed to add that as another life motto.

Grandma looked like a nutcracker as she kept opening her mouth and clamping it shut. She probably had so many opinions she couldn't figure out which one to voice first.

"Did either of you know Jason worked at the paint factory?" Hemi asked. "Because I didn't."

"No, or I would've asked him about Errol Danforth and Stan Stanton." In the past, I'd found his tendency to ramble had made him a good source.

"Jason was already working at the assembly plant when he and Rochelle started dating." Grandma dropped onto the couch.

My stomach twisted as another possibility slammed into me. "Do you think it's possible *Jason* murdered Morris Fulton and was the sniper?" I couldn't quite grasp that my brother-in-law would shoot Fulton in the back or target me like a doe in hunting season.

"Do you know where he was when both incidents happened?" Hemi paced in front of the chalkboard. "Does he own a gun?"

My mind tried to grasp details. "I never, in a million years, thought to ask either question, but he and Rochelle came home from the lake on Tuesday evening, so hypothetically, they were back in time for him to shoot Fulton on Wednesday."

"Does Rochelle have a key to your dad's office that Jason could've taken?" Hemi continued pacing.

"I'm not sure. At one point, Dad tried to convince her to come work in his office to help Eileen." I sat next to Grandma.

"Then, I'd say it's possible, no matter how much we don't want to believe it," he whispered.

"No way." Grandma scowled. "He's not capable of pulling something like this off. I'd have sensed it."

I didn't want to believe I'd been duped either, but we had to consider the facts in light of the new information. "I haven't had a chance to tell you this, Grandma, but last night, Jason was on the payphone outside the motel. He was shouting about being dragged into something and that he was 'squared up' and 'out.' When I asked what was up, he claimed he was calling his boss—at 2:30 in the morning."

"That could be true," Grandma said.

"But Jason acted defensive and said something about reports that sounded made up." I pointed at the board. "His conversation makes a lot more sense if he took hush money to ignore environmental violations."

"Since Jason mentioned being 'squared up' and wanting out, he might be trying to make things right now that his family's in danger," Hemi said.

"I hope so." I tried to put my swirling emotions aside and focus. "Let's take a step back. I don't see evidence that Jason was involved in framing Errol Danforth for armed robbery or killing anyone."

"And Rick wrote a question mark after the note about Danforth," Hemi said.

"That makes me feel better," Grandma muttered.

"Let's see what else we can find." I hopped up, opened a desk drawer, shuffled through pens and a stack of papers shoved haphazardly into the space. "Nothing."

Hemi threw open a closet, then faced us. "Rick is living with a woman." He pointed to women's clothing that took up about three-fourths of the closet space. The rest of the closet contained men's clothes.

I opened another desk drawer and removed a stack of papers secured with binder clips. On the top page was the title: *Wrongful Conviction: The Guy Baxter Story*.

What in the world?

"I don't think Rick's living here at all." I held up the manuscript. "My parents are."

CHAPTER 25

"If my parents are staying here, then they suspect Jason." I gripped the manuscript and stared at the chalkboard. "And how long have they known?"

"Jason might've taken hush money, but I still don't believe he'd harm a fly." Grandma took the manuscript and flipped through it. "Let's wait for Guy and Nicki and see what they know."

I glanced at my watch. "If we take too much longer to get back to the resort, Jason and Rochelle will get suspicious, and what are we going to say? 'Uhh . . . Jason, did you take a bribe, murder Morris Fulton, and try to kill me yesterday?'"

"Let's sit tight another ten minutes," Hemi said. "If they're not here by then, we can try tomorrow morning."

Hemi and I looked at Grandma, who nodded.

Hemi studied the chalkboard. "Mateo told us Rick was going undercover in another state, and we already suspected that Rick interviewed for a job at the paint factory. What if Rick was also the guy Teresa saw staking out Jason and Rochelle's house?" Hemi said. "He might've been following Jason to get information for your parents."

Following Jason.

A memory surfaced, and I snapped my fingers. “When we visited Rochelle at work, there was a guy reading on the bench outside the boutique. At the time, I thought he was waiting on his wife, but when we went inside, there wasn’t anyone shopping. I was so focused on talking to Rochelle that I didn’t put the pieces together until right now, but that guy was skinny and wearing sunglasses. If it was Rick, he might’ve been waiting for Jason to come out.”

“Now that you mention it, I vaguely remember seeing him, but I didn’t think much of it either,” Hemi said.

Outside, a car door slammed, and I flew to the window and pushed the curtain aside. Mom and Dad were getting out of a yellow VW Beetle. “They’re back.” A ripple of nervousness ran through my body. What would they say when they found us?

Outside, footfalls sounded on the steps as the tension in the apartment built. Grandma stepped forward and threw open the door. “Surprise.”

“Mom?” Shock registered on my mom’s face as she rushed inside.

“What’re you doing here?” Holding a grocery bag, Dad entered and locked the door behind him.

“Looking for answers, but now we have even more questions.” Grandma pointed over her shoulder at the chalkboard.

Dad pressed his lips together. I’d never seen him with a full beard, and because it was peppered with gray and he wore glasses, he looked much older. However, his broad chest and strong tattooed arms still gave him an imposing presence.

Mom threw her arms around me and smoothed my hair. She wore a peasant skirt and T-shirt, and she’d dyed her blond hair brown, but her blue eyes stood out behind her wire-rimmed glasses. “Are you okay? What about your sister and the baby?”

“We’re all fine.”

Mom hugged Grandma. When she raised her head, her questioning gaze fell on Hemi. "Nice to see you, Hemi."

"Hemi and Bobbi Sue are dating." Grandma patted Dad on the arm. "I vetted him for you. He's a good one." She winked at Hemi.

Dad grunted at Hemi as he set the sack on the counter. Then, he put his arm around me and kissed my cheek. "Good to see you, Bobbi Bear. We've missed you. You just took us by surprise."

"Please, sit." Mom pointed at the worn sofa in front of the window. "We need to talk."

That was an understatement.

Hemi, Grandma, and I lined up on the couch while Mom perched on the bed.

"Where's Rick?" Grandma asked. "We thought this was his apartment."

"It was, but he moved into the main house after he inherited it when his aunt died, so he's running his business from there to save on rent," Mom said.

I pointed at the chalkboard. "Has he been in Indiana recently—looking for evidence that Jason was involved in framing Errol Danforth?"

Mom and Dad exchanged glances.

"Yes, but it didn't start that way," Mom said. "Let me give Rick a call and see if he can join us. He came home yesterday afternoon." She reached for the phone next to the bed and dialed.

While she talked to Rick, Dad took a chair from the kitchen and straddled it. "Do Jason and Rochelle know you're here?" he asked.

"Sort of. They're at Goldenvale Resort and think we're getting groceries because we didn't tell them about looking for

Rick." When Mom hung up the phone, I told them about the sniper and fleeing Wildcat Springs with Jesse Joe's help.

Mom gasped. "Oh sweetie. How are you holding up?"

"A bullet grazed my arm, but other than that I'm fine." I shifted.

"Bobbi Bear . . ." Dad's face grew gray, but his eyes flashed with anger. "Why'd a sniper try to kill you?"

I told them about finding Morris Fulton, Juanita's arrest, and our investigation that'd led us to Florida.

"She's helped the sheriff's department solve a couple of murders this summer," Grandma said when I finished. "She'll make a top-notch reporter."

"We heard Fulton was murdered at your dad's office and that Juanita was arrested, but didn't realize you were so involved, Bobbi Sue," Mom said.

"I don't like you putting yourself in danger." Dad looked at me. "I don't like it at all."

Had it never occurred to them that their daughter, who wanted to be an investigative reporter, would try to find answers? I brushed the thought away. They'd had a lot on their minds.

Grandma snorted. "Well, that's the pot calling the kettle black. How long were you going to keep us in the dark about your dangerous exoneration hobby?" She looked back and forth between Mom and Dad. "Your daughters and I should've heard about it from you—not Juanita St. James."

"I was trying to protect you." Dad crossed his arms.

"Yet we find ourselves in danger," Grandma muttered.

Hemi held up a hand. "How about we keep sharing what we know, so we're on the same page moving forward?"

Hemi's peacemaking was a lifeline, and I knew that, without a doubt, I wanted to spend the rest of my life with this man. I couldn't logically explain why I was having such a revelation at this moment.

I just knew.

Grandma set her jaw. "Fine."

"Agreed," Dad said.

Mom nodded at Hemi as if she were thankful for his mediation. "Guy, why don't you start with the night we left?"

"Yep." Dad smoothed his beard. "That night, I got a call from someone using a voice changer who told me that if I didn't stop looking into Errol Danforth's case, I'd be arrested for Ross's murder. Since I'd found Ross's body at the inn's construction site a few days earlier, and I already suspected what someone with power on the inside had done to Danforth, I decided your mom and I had no choice but to run."

"Ever since your dad was exonerated, we'd had a contingency plan in case Victor Delacruz came after us," Mom said. "We took those IDs, the emergency cash, the fake license plate, threw some clothes in suitcases, and escaped to Michigan."

"We thought the less you and Rochelle knew, the better." Dad looked at me. "And your grandma was on a cruise. We didn't believe anyone would target you, since neither of you knew about my trying to exonerate the wrongfully convicted. I had no idea Fulton would come to Wildcat Springs and dig around in Errol Danforth's case when he didn't get those case files from me."

"Do you think Fulton was killed because he was investigating Danforth's case?" I asked.

"I have no doubt," Dad said. "Whoever is behind this doesn't want the truth getting out. This situation is bigger than I could've ever imagined."

"The folks calling the shots have to have help from local law enforcement," Grandma said.

Mom and Dad shared a look, and Mom said, "We agree, so we're not sure who to trust."

Thump. Thump. Thump.

Mom opened the door, and a man with sunglasses resting on his bald head entered. He wore a Hawaiian shirt, fit Stan's description of a shrimpy guy, and was definitely the man who'd been waiting outside of Margo's Boutique in Richardville.

"Nice to see you again," I said. "How was your visit to Indiana?"

"Not as productive as I'd hoped, but I hear you've been on the case," Rick said.

After Mom introduced everyone, she turned to Dad. "Explain why we decided to hire Rick."

"After a couple of weeks hiding out in Michigan, I started to feel awful about leaving Danforth hanging. I knew that unless I found the truth, we'd be on the run forever, so we came to Florida and hired Rick to investigate in my place," Dad said. "Rick can tell you the rest."

"When I went to Indiana, I visited Danforth in prison, and he told me that when Guy visited, he didn't want to incriminate anyone who took the hush money, so he didn't tell Guy about it," Rick said. "But after he heard Guy fled Wildcat Springs, Danforth changed his mind and told me Jason was involved. He had no idea Jason was Guy's son-in-law."

"Did Danforth tell you who else took money?" Grandma asked.

Rick shook his head. "Jason was the only one Danforth knew about, but he suspected there were others."

"What else did Danforth tell you?" Hemi asked.

"He thought the person making the payouts was a factory employee, but he didn't know who."

"Did you happen to be following Jason when Morris Fulton was killed on Wednesday afternoon?" I held my breath.

"I was," Rick said. "Jason may've taken hush money, but he was at work when Fulton was killed."

"Thank the Lord," I whispered.

"Well, hallelujah," Grandma muttered.

As relieved as I was, I wasn't feeling gracious toward my wayward brother-in-law. "Rick, when you were following Jason, did he ever meet with anyone unusual?"

"No. He acted nervous and squirrely, but I never got anything on him other than what Danforth told me."

"How do we fix this?" Grandma asked. "Danforth is in prison for a crime he didn't commit, Fulton's killer is on the loose, Juanita St. James is falsely accused, someone almost killed Bobbi Sue, Rochelle is married to a man with questionable morals, and my daughter and son-in-law are hiding out in Florida dressed like hippies who forgot that Woodstock ended almost twenty-years ago."

We sat in silence until I said, "We need to convince Jason to turn himself in."

"How can we do that if we can't trust our local law enforcement?" Mom asked.

"We'll contact Special Agent Erickson and tell him what we've uncovered," I said.

Dad rubbed the back of his neck. "How do you know him?"

I explained how the FBI agent had come to see me and asked about Fulton—and where my parents were. "For some reason, Fulton was already on the FBI's radar, or Special Agent Erickson never would've asked about him. Maybe they were already investigating the corruption at the paint factory."

"I'm not thrilled about trusting the feds, but it's looking like we don't have a better option since you've been targeted," Dad said. "What do you think, Rick?"

"I hit a lot of dead ends, so I'd say your son-in-law cooperating with the feds is the best bet."

Mom and Dad looked at each other, and finally Mom said, "Guy, it's time that Rochelle knows. We can't keep this from her forever. It's not fair."

"You're right—and Jason needs to be held accountable." Dad looked at his watch. "We'll give you a head start back to the resort since you came in a golf cart."

"I'm going with you and Nicki," Grandma said. "Hemi drives that golf cart like a race car, and I don't want to get thrown out and end up in the nursing home with a broken hip."

"I'm so sorry Grandma lied about your driving," I said as Hemi drove the golf cart around Lake Sereno on the way back to the resort.

"I know it's not about me." He slowed the cart for a bend in the path. "She wants to make sure your parents come to the villa."

"Yes, but she could've said that she'd help them find our villa or something that didn't make you look bad."

"In the scheme of things, it's not a big deal," he said. "To be honest, the look on your dad's face told me he was on to her."

That was probably true. "I'm still having trouble believing Jason is involved in this mess."

"Me too. I hope he's willing to come clean." He reached for my hand as we entered the resort's grounds.

After we rounded a curve in the path, our villa came into sight. A man stood on the porch pounding the front door. He glanced over his shoulder, though he didn't appear to notice us.

"Hemi," I whispered. "That's my dad's foreman, Bruce."

"I know." He squeezed my hand. "This can't be good."

As Hemi slowed the golf cart to a stop in the driveway, Rochelle opened the door. "Bruce? What're you doing here?"

CHAPTER 26

"HEY, Rochelle. I need to see Jason," Bruce said as Hemi and I got out of the golf cart. "It's important."

"But . . . you came to Florida? I don't understand how you knew we're here." Fear tinged her voice as she clutched the door frame for support, and when she looked past Bruce and saw Hemi and me, relief showed on her face.

"This is my mother-in-law's resort, and I'm on vacation with my family. This afternoon, I was paddle boating on the lake when I thought I saw Bobbi Sue, Hemi, and your grandma drive by on a golf cart. I asked Marion, and she confirmed you flew in this afternoon."

I curled my fingers. So much for being discreet. Grandma was right. Marion *was* bad news.

"From what I heard from contractors back home, it was a last-minute vacation," I said.

"Hey, there." Bruce glanced over his shoulder. "It was. I needed to get my family out of Wildcat Springs."

"Why?" Rochelle asked.

Another piece fell into place as I remembered what Jesse Joe had told us. Bruce had worked at the factory. He must've taken hush money, and now he was in danger too. I glanced at Hemi and saw understanding in his expression.

"May I please talk to Jason?" Bruce asked. "It's important."

"He's out running, but you can come in and wait on him." Rochelle stepped aside, and Bruce entered the villa. Hemi and I followed, and I locked the door behind us.

"Would you like anything to drink?" Rochelle asked.

"No thanks." Bruce glanced at his watch. "How much longer do you think Jason will be?"

"He's been gone about a half hour, so he should be back soon." Rochelle glanced at me, her eyes full of questions. "Why don't you have a seat?" She pointed toward the living room. Bruce sat but bounced his leg.

"Where's Jesse Joe?" I murmured.

Rochelle didn't take her eyes off Bruce. "On a walk."

As Rochelle, Hemi, and I settled on the couch, my mind swirled while I pieced together Bruce's involvement. Juanita had sensed something was off about him when he'd stopped at my house the night Fulton had been shot, and now I needed to see if Bruce would talk. "While we're waiting for Jason, do you mind if I ask you a few questions?"

He checked his watch—again. "Go ahead."

"Before you came to work for my dad, did you work with Jason at Richardville Paint Factory?" I asked.

"Yep." He crossed his arms.

"When the new owners took over, did they cut corners on environmental and safety regulations?"

"Yep."

"Did you accept a bribe to ignore the violations?"

"Yep."

"Do you know if Jason also accepted a bribe?"

"He did, which is why you're in this mess." Bruce stared out the patio door—unable to look at my sister.

"What're you saying, Bobbi Sue?" Color drained from Rochelle's face.

"Bruce and Jason took payouts from the new owners to stay quiet, but Errol Danforth refused, so someone set him up for armed rob—"

"Jason wouldn't do that!" Rochelle's face grew red as she glared at me and then faced Bruce. "Tell her!"

"We had nothing to do with framing Danforth." Bruce hung his head. "He was a good guy—a lot better than Jason and me."

Rochelle moaned and buried her face in her hands, but when I rested my hand on her back, she shook it off.

"Who arranged the payments for you and Jason?" Hemi asked.

"A mysterious entity known as the Broker." Bruce glanced at the door. "I'm convinced the Broker framed Danforth."

"Did you look at the court transcripts in Danforth's case?" I asked.

He tilted his head. "How'd you know?"

I told him.

"Well, I didn't find anything that pointed to the Broker, but I had to try," Bruce said. "I thought the eyewitnesses' stories were a little too perfect."

"And they're both dead," Hemi added.

Bruce met his eyes. "I know."

Rochelle moaned.

"What else can you tell us about the Broker?" I asked.

"Not much—except this person has eyes everywhere. I don't even know if the Broker is male or female, because we never met in person," Bruce said. "They used a voice changer and gave me instructions on where to pick up the cash. A few months after I took the bribe, I went to work for your dad and hadn't heard from the Broker in years until about a month ago."

"Do you think the Broker reached out because Errol

Danforth wanted my dad to investigate his case, and Dad asked questions that tipped off the people behind this scheme?"

"I think so," Bruce said. "The Broker tried damage control to get your dad to back off, and it worked—until Morris Fulton picked up where Guy left off. Ever since the FBI started sniffing around, things have been unraveling fast."

"I'm so lost right now." Rochelle raised her head. "What do you mean, 'damage control to get Dad to back off?'"

"The Broker convinced Dad that he'd be blamed for Ross Garland's murder if he kept trying to prove Danforth had been wrongfully convicted," I said.

"And Dad believed it because of his history," Rochelle whispered. "That's the real reason he and Mom left."

"The Broker has to have law enforcement connections in Richard County—but I don't have proof," Bruce said.

Hemi and I exchanged glances.

The door rattled, and Jason stepped inside. His running shirt was sweat-soaked, and his face glistened. "Bruce? What're you doing here? What's going on?"

"He told us you took a bribe from that evil Broker person!" Rochelle screeched.

Jason's face went gray. "Sweetie, let me expl—"

"Jason, you can smooth things over later," Bruce said. "The Broker might've followed you from Wildcat Springs, so we need to talk before I take my family and split."

CHAPTER 27

"How'd you find us?" Jason glared at Bruce.

Bruce told him. "Before I leave, I wanted to tell you I've been working with FBI Special Agent Cole Erickson. He's trying to take down the Broker, and I agreed to be a witness in exchange for immunity. You should do the same. It's the only way out of this mess." Bruce checked his watch. "I've got to get my family out of here, but if I were you, I'd make a deal while there's time." He took a business card from his pocket. "This is Special Agent Erickson's contact information."

Jason took the card. "Thanks."

Bruce surveyed us. "Be safe." Then, he hurried out the door.

Jason's shoulders drooped, and he looked back at Rochelle, who refused to meet his eyes. I was relieved that Bruce had done the hard job of telling Rochelle about Jason's involvement and hoped Bruce's encouragement would get Jason to cooperate with Special Agent Erickson.

"Rochelle, there's something else you should know," I said.

"No!" She buried her head in her hands. "I can't take more bad news."

"We found Mom and Dad, and they're on their way here with Grandma."

"What?" She lifted her head.

I explained what Grandma, Hemi, and I had been doing while she and Jason were at the pool and what we'd learned from Mom, Dad, and Rick.

After I finished, Rochelle squeezed the bridge of her nose, before drilling Jason with her gaze. "Explain yourself."

"I was young and made a stupid mistake before we even started dating, and it caught up with me all these years later," Jason said. "I'm sorry. I'm so, so, sorry."

"I don't want to hear you're sorry." Rochelle's measured words held a note of underlying fury. "I want. An explanation."

"Okay, okay." He ran his hands through his hair. "Back in 1985, Errol Danforth and I figured out that the factory wasn't disposing of chemicals the right way, and Errol wanted to blow the whistle," Jason said. "I was with him until I got a note in my locker offering money if I kept quiet. I had to call a number for instructions. Errol got a note too, but he refused to call. I had credit card debt, so I called the number, and someone used a voice changer to tell me to pick up the money at a bus station locker in Richardville. There was ten grand in cash in the bag. I'd never seen that much money in my life, and I used it to pay off my debt."

He looked at Rochelle, but her face remained expressionless.

"How long have you known Bruce took the money?" Hemi asked.

"Since a few days after Errol was arrested for robbing a convenience store," Jason said. "I was so upset over the news that Bruce noticed, and when we got to talking, he admitted he'd taken the bribe and was freaking out too."

"You were upset because you suspected Danforth had been framed for not going along with the bribe?" I asked.

"Right. I know I'm not a genius, but it wasn't hard to connect the dots. If Danforth needed money, why not take ten grand the easy way instead of robbing a convenience store? But I couldn't say anything because there was a note in the money bag telling me that if I ever said a word about the money, I'd pay."

"You let an innocent man go to prison," Rochelle said.

"We didn't know Danforth that well, and Bruce and I speculated that we were wrong, and he got drunk and did something out of character. Besides, the robbery had eyewitnesses, and he had a trial!"

"So did my dad, and we know how that went!" Rochelle shouted. "All this time, did you know the real reason my parents left?"

"I suspected." Jason hung his head. "After your dad looked into Danforth's case, the Broker contacted me for ideas on how to get your dad to back off. I knew he'd found Ross Garland's body, so I gave the Broker the idea."

"You let me worry for weeks that my parents were hiding from a vengeful drug lord when you were partly responsible for them leaving. Did you take money for selling Dad out?" Rochelle asked.

"No." Jason flinched. "I figured if I cooperated, the Broker would leave us alone for good. I had no idea your parents would run. I figured your dad would stop investigating Danforth's case and that would be that."

Funny how he'd thought that'd satisfy a criminal.

Hemi glanced at me before turning to Jason. "Do you have any idea who the Broker could be?"

"No, but I've always suspected the Broker worked at the paint factory," Jason said. "It had to be someone with easy access to our lockers."

"Jason, when I overheard you on the payphone, were you talking to the Broker?" I asked.

"Yes. When I left work last night, there was a note on my

car's dashboard telling me to call from a payphone within twenty-four hours, or I'd be sorry," Jason said. "The Broker laughed at my offer to pay back the money with interest. I know too much—and not enough."

That was a surprisingly deep statement from Jason.

I bit my lip and thought about the Broker using a voice changer. "A voice changer modifies the person's pitch, but it can't hide speech patterns, unique expressions—or even background noise. Did you happen to notice anything like that during the phone calls?"

Jason scrunched his face. "Not that I can think of, but I'll keep trying to remember."

"I hate to be morbid, but does anyone else wonder why the Broker didn't kill Danforth instead of framing him?" Hemi asked. "Especially if that same person killed Morris Fulton and tried to take out Bobbi Sue?"

Rochelle clutched a pillow to her chest. "It's possible making Danforth suffer from a wrongful conviction was worse than death."

"Or the Broker cared about Danforth at one time and wanted to spare his life," Hemi said. "That would explain why he wasn't killed, but Fulton was."

"Or the Broker, Fulton's killer, and the sniper aren't the same person," I said.

We lapsed into silence, and when the door rattled, Rochelle and I jumped.

But Grandma and Jesse Joe entered—alone.

"Where are Mom and Dad?" Rochelle asked. "Bobbi Sue and Hemi told me everything. Including what he did." She pointed at Jason.

Grandma came over to the couch and sat next to Rochelle. "How're you feeling?" Grandma rubbed my sister's back.

"I'm not sure." Rochelle glared at Jason. "Where are Mom and Dad?"

"After Bobbi Sue and Hemi left, I told your parents the Goldenvale Resort owner has Richardville connections, and that made them nervous. We decided it was best for them to stay put. No sense in blowing their covers now," Grandma said. "So, I hoofed it back here and ran into Jesse Joe on the way."

"Izzy told me what you were doing while I was lazing at the pool," Jesse Joe said.

"Grandma, you made the right call telling Mom and Dad about Marion." I told them about Bruce's visit and how Marion had confirmed we were here. "He's terrified the Broker followed us from Indiana, so he took his family and left."

Grandma looked at Jesse Joe. "Then we can't stay here either."

"I know. Just tell me where you want to go, and I'll fly you there." Jesse Joe appeared sheepish. "I should've thought about the connections, but Marion had been pestering me to visit, so when you said you needed to go to Honeybell, I thought I had the perfect solution. I also didn't realize Marion might have ulterior motives." His cheeks colored.

Grandma smirked. "We'll leave first thing in the morning and figure out where to go when we get to the airport. Let's try to get some sleep."

"Will do." Jesse Joe reached over, squeezed Grandma's hand, and went to his bedroom.

"I-I guess I'll be on the couch tonight." Jason reached for a throw pillow.

"You guessed right," Rochelle snapped.

The next morning, Marion insisted on driving us to the airport in the resort van. No one had anything to say as we piled inside, and the tension between Rochelle and Jason was palpable. The night before, I hadn't slept more than a couple of hours, and the sounds of my sister's sobs had filtered through the wall. Grandma had checked on her but quickly returned to our room.

"Rochelle needs to be alone and process," she'd said.

As Marion drove the highway looping Lake Sereno, she cast a furtive glance at Jesse Joe, who was sitting in the passenger seat. "I'm so sorry it didn't work out for you to stay longer, but you'll have to come back another time."

"We'll see," he said.

It was clear from Jesse Joe's tone that *we'll see* really meant *heck no*, but I wasn't confident that Marion would take the hint. I glanced at Grandma sitting next to me and caught her triumphant smirk. Hemi tapped my foot as amusement danced in his eyes.

"Where are you folks headed?" Marion glanced in the rearview mirror.

That was a good question because if Grandma and Jesse Joe had discussed it, they hadn't share with the rest of us.

"Somewhere safe," Grandma said. "And far away from Richard County."

Marion nodded. "I've heard some wild stories from my family and friends back in Indiana. I used to think Richard County was a haven, but now I'm glad I don't live there."

Since Marion was the only one who seemed to want to talk, I figured we should take advantage of that. "What have you heard?"

"For starters, I've heard there's been an uptick in murders in cute little Wildcat Springs, of all places."

"That's true," I said.

"You know my daughter and son-in-law were staying with

me at Goldenvale, and I got the distinct feeling that they're running from something back home, but I couldn't get my daughter to talk. They left last night as abruptly as they came." She shook her head. "I was hoping for more time with my grandkids."

I glanced at Jason, and he was fidgeting with his seatbelt.

Marion flipped on the turn signal as she approached the airport entrance. "I get letters from my friend Teresa asking for prayer for her brother because she's certain he was put in prison for a crime he didn't commit."

"Teresa Hawkins?" I asked.

"That's right." Marion glanced back at me. "How do you know her?"

"She's our neighbor," Rochelle said.

"What a small world! She attended the church where my husband and I served. I've been after her to come and visit. If you tell her that you enjoyed your stay, she'll be more likely to make the trip. That is—if you enjoyed your stay."

"We did." Rochelle flashed a smile that I knew was forced. "It was just too short."

Marion stopped the van next to the terminal entrance. "Well, here we are." She rested a hand on Jesse Joe's shoulder. "Don't be a stranger." She batted her eyes.

"Thanks for your hospitality," Jesse Joe mumbled as he scrambled to unbuckle his seatbelt and escape.

Somehow, I didn't think Grandma needed to fear Marion's wiles.

Grandma, Hemi, Rochelle, Jason, and I waited in the terminal while Jesse Joe inspected and readied his plane. We'd found a group of chairs in a corner where we had a view of the runway.

Rochelle sat with her arms crossed and was using Grandma and me as her buffer.

Finally, Jason cleared his throat. "I, uh, have something to say."

We turned toward him.

"I'm sorry for the trouble I brought to your family." Jason twisted his wedding band. "I'm going to do everything in my power to make things right, and as soon as we're in a safe place, I'll call Special Agent Erickson and do what I can to help stop the Broker."

"I'm glad to hear that," Grandma said.

Rochelle remained expressionless, and Hemi patted Jason on the shoulder. Outside, Jesse Joe taxied toward the terminal, so we filed to the door. When we passed a middle-aged couple with a fluffy white dog in a travel crate, the dog emitted a low growl.

"Easy there, killer," Grandma muttered.

We boarded the plane, and as Grandma climbed into the cockpit next to Jesse Joe, she asked, "Did you inspect this bird well? I don't think the Broker's found us, but damaging our plane would be a good way to take us out."

"I know." Jesse Joe said. "I went over everything three times, and I didn't see anything wrong. I even thought like a criminal and made sure nobody tampered with the fuel."

Rochelle blew out a breath. "That makes me feel better."

Rochelle and I sat in the middle seats while Hemi kept an eye on Jason in the back. We put on our headsets, and Jesse Joe taxied toward the runway.

"Um, I just remembered something about the Broker," Jason said into his headset.

"What?" Hemi and I asked in unison.

"That fluffy white dog that growled at us jogged my memory." Jason leaned forward. "Years ago, the money bag I picked up from the bus station had some white hairs in it. At the time, I figured it was from a dog or a cat. Then, during my last call with the Broker, I heard a dog yapping in the background, and the barking got so bad the Broker said, 'Shut up, Velda.'"

A white dog named Velda—not exactly the most common pet name.

I turned and met Hemi's wide eyes.

"Jane White from Willow Haven is the Broker," we said in unison.

CHAPTER 28

As Jesse Joe waited on the runway for our plane to be cleared for takeoff, I considered the pieces to see if they made sense. I faced Jason. "Do you know if a woman named Jane White ever worked at Richardville Paint Factory? Because she has a white dog named Velda."

Jason gazed out the window. "Seems like there was a Jane who worked in human resources, but I don't think her last name was White."

Then, I remembered. "She took her maiden name back—after she divorced Sheriff Carter."

"That's her," Jason said. "Jane Carter. She had a chip on her shoulder and always acted like anybody with a question was bothering her."

"She bit my head off once when I asked about insurance," Jesse Joe said, then refocused on flying when the tower cleared us for takeoff.

"Do you think Jane worked with Sheriff Carter to frame Danforth even though they were divorced?" Hemi asked.

"They were probably still married at the time. They split fairly recently." Grandma's eyes clouded. "I've never trusted that man, and I've always thought the people of Richard County would regret electing him. This case only makes sense if law enforcement is involved in the cover-ups."

"It explains why Sheriff Carter has been more involved in the Fulton murder investigation and why they were quick to pin everything on Juanita." I glanced out the window as the plane gained speed. "For all we know, Sheriff Carter put pressure on Detective Harrell to make an arrest."

"All this time, I've wondered why Morris Fulton rented a townhouse in Wildcat Springs," Hemi said. "But if he suspected Jane White set up Errol Danforth, then living in her building would be the perfect opportunity to spy on her and prove that she was involved."

"Willow Haven is within walking distance of Dad's office, so if Jane figured out what Fulton was doing, she must've followed him and confronted him there." As the plane lifted off the ground, I considered Jane's friendship with Teresa. "Jane set up her best friend's little brother for armed robbery. The same little brother she used to babysit. That's cold."

"But it explains why Jane didn't off Danforth," Grandma said.

The plane continued to climb, and the runway ended. But a movement on the ground caught my eye. A figure dressed in camouflage emerged from the bushes and aimed a rifle at the plane.

I gasped. "Sniper!"

A second later, a sickening metallic clank jolted the fuselage, and the engine's steady hum wavered—then sputtered. The floor buzzed underneath my sandals.

Rochelle screamed, and I gripped my seat as the plane grew eerily quiet. To our right, neat rows of trees blurred past. An orange grove? To the east was a large grassy area.

Jesse Joe swore and checked the gauges. "I gotta put us down in that clearing."

"Dear Lord, help us," Grandma whispered.

The plane's nose dipped slightly, and the wind rushed around us as tremors shook the plane.

"Brace for impact!" Jesse Joe shouted.

I ducked, covered my head, and prayed the plane wouldn't catch fire.

The plane slammed to the ground with a thud and bounced, jarring my body. As the plane bounced a second time, my seatbelt dug into my hips. Our purses and books tumbled on the floor. My groans mingled with everyone's whimpers and shouts of pain. The plane skidded over rough grass, and as much as I wanted to look up, I was afraid to raise my head.

Please stop, please stop, please stop.

At last, the skidding slowed to a crawl, and the plane stilled as dust drifted around us. With ringing ears, I raised my head. We'd come to a stop within a few feet of pine trees. Grandma and Jesse Joe were stirring in the cockpit. Rochelle groaned beside me. I whipped around, and Hemi coughed but nodded. The color in Jason's face had vanished.

"I-Is everyone okay?" I asked.

"Maybe," Grandma said.

"Pretty sure my leg's broken." Jesse Joe moaned and tried the radio. After a few attempts, he said, "Radio's dead."

Hemi squeezed between Rochelle and me. "We need to get out in case of a fire." He shoved the door until it snapped open, and humid air rushed in. He hopped out and held out his hand. Grasping it, I stepped onto the ground on shaky legs and helped my sister out.

"Take cover away from the plane," Hemi said. "Jason and I will help your grandma and Jesse Joe."

With Rochelle leaning against me, we staggered across the field toward the orange grove and ducked between the tree rows. I helped her sit on the ground and lean against a tree with small green oranges.

"That impact was awful—it can't have been good for the baby." She pressed her hands to her abdomen. "Everything happened so fast."

"Are you cramping?" I asked.

"No." She pushed hair from her face as tears welled in her eyes. "Do you think the sniper was Jane White?"

I remembered Jane's Army shirt and her dog's camo-print collar. "It's possible since she may've served in the Army." I surveyed our deserted surroundings in the orange grove. Though we weren't far from the airport, Jesse Joe hadn't had time for a mayday call before the radio died. Would anyone realize we'd crashed?

Would the sniper hunt us?

I slipped between the trees and looked back at the plane. Hemi helped Grandma out, and I waved. She trudged toward the grove, and I hurried to meet her, but she shooed me away.

"Stay under cover," she shouted as she picked her way across the field. "I can make it."

I waited at the grove's edge while Hemi disappeared into the plane, and I prayed that I wouldn't see it ignite into a fireball. Seconds crawled until Jason emerged and helped Hemi maneuver Jesse Joe out of the plane. Once they were on the ground, Hemi and Jason supported Jesse Joe as he hobbled toward us.

Grandma and I joined Rochelle, and when my sister stood, Grandma opened her arms and gathered us in a hug. "That was one of the scariest experiences of my life."

To our left was a gravel road, and I heard the puttering of an approaching motor. A man in a wide-brimmed hat was driving a red open-cab tractor. "I'll flag him down." I jogged between the rows while waving my arms, and the farmer stopped and got off the tractor.

"What's going on, miss?" His leathery tan made his blue eyes stand out.

"Please call for help. Our plane crashed in the field next to the grove." I pointed, though the trees blocked his view. "Our pilot didn't have time to make a Mayday call, so I don't know if anyone at the airport knows we crashed."

"Will do. My wife and I live up the road." He pointed at a white stucco cottage behind him. "Is anyone hurt?"

"Yes."

"Can you folks hang on 'til help arrives?"

I bit my lip. "I think so."

He climbed onto his tractor and puttered to his house while I trudged through the tunnel of trees to Grandma and Rochelle. When a breeze ruffled the leaves, the sun caught the reflection of something at the end of the row, and I stopped.

"What's wrong, Bobbi Sue?" Rochelle asked.

I shaded my eyes. "There's something at the end of the row."

Before they could stop me or I could change my mind, I jogged down there, and a black car's chrome bumper came into view. The car was wedged between the grove's edge and a large saw palmetto.

Was this the sniper's getaway vehicle?

It had a Georgia license plate, and I whispered the numbers aloud three times to commit them to memory. A small sticker on the corner of the windshield had a rental car company logo.

This had to be the sniper's car because no one else would have a logical reason to park here. I needed to do something—fast.

The tires.

Glancing around, I didn't see anyone coming, so I darted to the car, knelt next to a tire, and unscrewed the valve cap.

Swiping a stick from the ground, I pressed on the valve until air swooshed out. I peeked over my shoulder while air hissed out, though the tire wasn't visibly deflated.

A vehicle whizzed by on the road beside me, but I didn't hear any sirens. Had the farmer not called for help?

At last, the tire sagged, so I replaced the cap, moved to the rear tire, and repeated the process. When that tire drooped, I screwed the cap back on.

Behind me, a twig popped, and I whipped around.

The masked shooter was aiming a rifle at me.

CHAPTER 29

"STEP AWAY FROM THE CAR," a woman said. Her pants were torn, her knees bloodied, and she swayed.

A fall must've slowed her escape.

I raised both hands and hoped she hadn't seen me deflating the tires. For now, they were hidden on the other side of the vehicle.

"Take off the mask, Jane. I know you're the Broker—and that you killed Morris Fulton and framed Errol Danforth."

Keeping her rifle aimed at me, she ripped off her mask with one hand. "I've heard you want to be an investigative reporter. Too bad you won't live long enough, because you're pretty good." She regripped her rifle with both hands and aimed at my chest.

I needed to keep her distracted. "How'd you find us?"

"That resort owner Marion was bellyaching to our mutual friend Teresa that Isadora Spearman was threatening her plan to snag that old widower Jesse Joe Darlington, and Teresa blabbed to me because she knows I knew Jesse Joe from the Richardville Paint Factory."

Grandma's instincts had been right again. "Why'd you become the Broker?"

"Respect—and power." Jane narrowed her eyes. "It's a man's world, and I'm tired of being a second-class citizen. I dealt with it in the military, and when I got a job at the factory, it was more of the same, even though I worked in human resources. Harassment. Looks. Suggestive comments."

"I get the concept of a man's world. I'm a waitress, and some men think my backside is fair game."

Jane scowled. "Men are pigs, sister, but I'm still gonna have to kill you."

I should've known I'd never be able to find common ground with a psycho. Better keep asking questions. "How'd you go from working in human resources to being the Broker?"

"When the new owners came in and cut corners, I saw an opportunity and volunteered to work behind the scenes to shut up the workers who were squawking about illegal dumping." She sneered. "Turns out, I was good at it, so I became their official fixer—and now they rely on me to make problems go away at their other factories in other states."

"That's a powerful position."

"And the money's nice. I have an offshore account that'll fund my retirement in the Caribbean. Right now, no one suspects because I just live in a simple townhouse. Nothing fancy or conspicuous, but my day to cash in is coming."

"But your cushy retirement plan was threatened when my dad investigated Errol Danforth's case."

Jane narrowed her eyes. "Errol was a sweet kid, but he should've just taken the money. We had to stop him from blowing the whistle."

"Yet you couldn't quite bring yourself to kill your best friend's little brother, so you set him up for armed robbery instead."

"He's not serving a life sentence and should be grateful we didn't kill him."

That made it all better. "You said *we*. Did your ex-husband help you frame Errol?"

"He was my worthless husband at the time, but he came through in that situation and helped me plant the evidence and find the witnesses to testify against Errol." She snorted. "But I can assure you, he did it for the money—not for me." She adjusted her grip on the rifle. "We'll be going to separate islands when the time comes. I'm not spending my golden years on the same rock as that toothpick sucker."

I nearly lost the battle to stop a laugh, but I took a shaky breath and asked, "Why'd you contact the workers who'd taken the money before? That was risky."

"When your dad started asking questions about Danforth, we knew it wouldn't be long until he figured out his son-in-law and foreman had taken bribes, so I offered more money to keep quiet and even got Jason to give me a suggestion on how to get your dad to stop investigating."

"But you never counted on Morris Fulton."

"I did what I had to do," she said. "I'm not losing everything I've worked for."

Just then, Hemi emerged from the woods behind her.

Praying a reaction hadn't shown on my face, I blurted, "Did you learn to be a sniper in the military?"

Hemi crept closer and grabbed a thick branch that he held like a baseball bat.

She scoffed. "Good one. When I served, I was stuck doing payroll. I learned from my brother who was a Green Beret."

"I bet that made for some interesting family holidays." I let loose a hysterical laugh and prayed that it'd cover the sound of Hemi approaching behind her.

"Yes." She rolled her eyes. "We were chipmunk assassins."

Hemi stopped, took a backswing, and I dove for cover as the branch thumped her body.

Jane screeched and cussed. When I lifted my head, Hemi was sitting on her back. The rifle lay on the ground out of her reach, but she wiggled as if she could worm her way to it.

I moved it away while Hemi removed his belt and secured her hands. She shrieked when I wrapped my belt around her ankles.

When I heard a vehicle approaching, I pushed aside the palmetto leaves and waved at the sheriff's deputy's vehicle. Meanwhile, Jane spewed her ugly thoughts about Hemi—and all men.

She could keep her crazed feminism. I was thrilled to have a man come to my rescue.

CHAPTER 30

THAT EVENING, Grandma, Hemi, Rochelle, Jason and I sat in the surgery waiting room in an Orlando hospital where Jesse Joe had been transported to have surgery on his broken leg. With our pilot—and plane—out of commission, we were stuck in Florida until tomorrow afternoon when we'd booked a commercial flight to Indianapolis. Grandma planned to stay with Jesse Joe—until Penny arrived.

We'd turned on an episode of *MacGyver* since we were the only ones waiting, but I couldn't focus. I ran my fingernail over my empty foam cup. The coffee hadn't done much to warm me in the air conditioning, so I leaned closer to Hemi, and he put his arm around me.

Grandma was once again sitting as a buffer between Jason and Rochelle, and they'd gone back to not speaking after finding out their baby was okay.

After we'd caught Jane that morning, Hemi and I had given our statements to the local sheriff and put him in contact with Special Agent Erickson. Jason had also reached out to the FBI agent, so when he strolled into the waiting room, I wasn't surprised.

"Good evening, Ms. Baxter." Special Agent Erickson scrutinized me. "I hear you had an exciting morning." He sat in the chair across from me.

"That's one way of putting it," Grandma muttered.

"Everyone, this is Special Agent Cole Erickson." *Should I introduce them individually?*

Before I could decide, Grandma said, "I'm Isadora Spearman." Then she pointed at everyone. "Hemi Miller, my granddaughter Rochelle, and her husband Jason. *McKeever*." Grandma eyed Erickson.

Erickson surveyed Jason, who stood. "Have a seat, Mr. McKeever. We'll chat after I finish talking with Bobbi Sue."

Jason quickly sat.

Erickson turned back to me. "I have to commend you for capturing Jane White. She's part of a multi-state crime network tied to the Richardville Paint Factory's owners. We've been working to dismantle that crime ring for a while, and now that we've caught Jane, that'll be a lot easier. She's naming names to save her own skin."

That I could believe. "Did she tell you Sheriff Carter in Richard County is involved?"

"Yes, she explained that her ex-husband helped her frame Danforth. The factory owners funded the payouts to her, the sheriff, and the fake witnesses," Special Agent Erickson said. "They paid off workers so they wouldn't blow the whistle on the illegal dumping."

Jason ducked his head.

"What made you visit me at Chuckie's last week and ask about my dad and Morris Fulton?" I asked.

"Before Fulton decided to come to Wildcat Springs, he reached out to us through an old prison contact. He suspected factory ties to Danforth's case but couldn't find proof. We think that's what he was looking for in Wildcat Springs and that he'd hoped your dad might've found something that he'd hidden in his office."

I nodded. "We thought Fulton was searching for proof too."

Grandma crossed her arms. "What about Juanita St. James? And Danforth? You gonna spring them?"

"It's already in the works," Erickson said. "Danforth will be out soon, and Juanita was released this afternoon. She's staying at your parents' house."

"What about our parents?" Rochelle asked. "When can they come home?"

"Whenever they're ready. Richard County should be safe again now that Jane, her ex-husband, and the factory owners are in custody." Special Agent Erickson stood. "Please reach out if you need anything else."

"We will," I said.

"All right, Mr. McKeever. I understand you wanted to talk to me." He motioned for Jason to follow, and as they left the waiting room, I rested my head on Hemi's shoulder.

I couldn't wait to get home and get back to normal.

CHAPTER 31

A FEW DAYS LATER, everyone was home safely in Wildcat Springs, including Mom and Dad. Dad got back to his construction business, and Mom was preparing her elementary classroom for a new school year. Juanita had decided to take more time off and was staying with us and enjoying the peacefulness of Wildcat Woods. Grandma was back in Indiana but talked to Jesse Joe on the phone every day.

Jason and Bruce were cooperating with the FBI and would probably avoid jail time, though Jason's relationship with my sister needed work. I hoped with time and counseling, they could move past everything that'd happened.

Since Misty had been dying to get details about my adventure, I agreed to meet her that evening at Tate's Place. When I walked in, "The Glory of Love" was playing on the jukebox, and I hummed along with Peter Cetera as I joined her at the bar where she was talking to Kurt.

Misty leaped from her stool and threw her arms around me. "I can't believe you were in a plane crash." She stepped back and kept her hands on my arms. "You could've died!"

"I'm aware."

"Glad you survived, Bobbi Snoop." Kurt filled a glass with Coke and handed it to me. "On the house."

"Thanks." I took the glass.

"I want all the details." Misty motioned for me to follow her to a booth. "But first, I have some news. Wanna guess?" She glanced back at the bar.

"You and Kurt are finally going on a date?"

She stuck out her lip. "How'd you guess so quickly?"

"Because you glanced at Kurt—and clearly wanted to have this conversation where he wouldn't hear."

"Well, you're partially right." She jutted her chin. "We've *been* on a date. Last night we went to a movie in Richardville."

"Is there going to be another?"

"Tomorrow. He wants to take me to Salvador's for Italian food." She scooted into a booth. "What's going on with you and Hemi?"

"We're still together. Even after everything—I didn't scare him away."

"That's good because if you're going to be an investigative reporter, he'll have to get used to you being in danger."

I set my glass on the table. "About that. I've been thinking a lot about my future, and I've decided I don't want to be the next Juanita St. James."

"What?" Misty's jaw dropped. "But what about your crusade for truth?"

"I can finish my degree and be a reporter who tells the truth. I don't have to be an *investigative* reporter."

She leaned back and studied me. "Why the change of heart?"

"Because two things can be true. As much as I want to be a journalist, I also want to be a wife and mother, and I don't want a career that's constantly putting me—or the people I love—in danger. This summer was so full of scary situations. I don't want to spend my life like that."

"Telling the truth can be dangerous," Misty said.

"I know. So, I could use my skills to do freelance writing if I have kids instead of working full time as a reporter." I shifted. "Let's just say I'm open to other options."

"You'll make a difference as a reporter—or a freelance writer," she said. "You've faced several lifetimes of danger in one summer." She raised her beer mug. "Here's to finishing college, marrying Hemi, and having babies."

I clinked her mug with my glass. "Cheers." I sipped my Coke.

"Wow." She giggled. "Since you drank to that without protest, I *know* you're serious about him." She looked around, then lowered her voice to a whisper. "On that note, let's drink to getting along with Amanda since she'll probably be your mother-in-law someday." Misty held up her mug.

I grimaced, then laughed. "Here, here."

The next evening, Mom and Dad had a cookout for Juanita, who was leaving for Chicago the next morning. Grandma and Hemi joined us, along with Rochelle. Jason was still welcome, but he couldn't join us because he had to work.

Dad fired up the grill, and Mom had citronella candles burning. Every so often, the bug zapper sizzled an insect.

"How's Jesse Joe doing?" I asked Grandma as I dealt placemats onto the table.

"That old coot is tough." She set the salt and pepper shakers on the table. "He's gonna be fine, though he's itching to get back home."

"Speaking of home," Mom came outside holding a platter stacked with hamburger patties. "I talked to Penny today, and she told me the camp sold. Jesse Joe had been thinking about moving to Grand Rapids, but Penny says he's going to move home to Richard County—maybe even Wildcat Springs." She waggled her eyebrows at Grandma and handed the burgers to Dad.

"Well." Grandma waved a hand, but her cheeks looked a little pink. "Being closer to his lifelong friends makes sense. It had to be boring living in that deserted old camp by himself." She bustled around the table and arranged silverware on the placemats.

Hemi and I grinned at each other.

Juanita cracked open a can of Sprite and leaned against the railing. "Now that Errol Danforth is getting out of prison, do you have another wrongful conviction case to investigate, Guy?"

Dad turned from the grill and glanced at Mom. "Nicki and I decided it'd be best if I give that up. I have some catching up to do on construction projects, and there are other ways to fight the good fight."

"How so?" Juanita asked.

Mom smiled. "Guy, do you want to share your news?"

Dad put a burger on the grill. "I have a contract to get my book published. Penny thought my story would sell, so Nicki and I wrote it while we were hiding out. Well, Nicki did most of the work. I just talked."

"That's not true," Mom said. "You relived your awful memories."

"Congratulations," Grandma said. "I'm glad you're giving up that investigation nonsense, but the world needs to hear your story."

"You're a big part of it, Juanita," Mom said.

"I appreciate that, but after what you did to help me, we can call it even." Juanita turned to Rochelle. "How's the baby?"

My sister nodded. "Fine. I don't seem to be having trouble—

after everything." She twisted her wedding ring. "My baby is a fighter."

"Just like you," Grandma said.

Hemi met my eyes. "Just like her entire family."

Later that evening, while Mom, Dad, Grandma, Rochelle, and Juanita reminisced on the deck, Hemi and I slipped away for a walk. Before we left, we stopped in the garage.

"This reminds me of our first outing." He opened the cabinet, took out the bug repellant, and handed it to me.

I sprayed myself. "When you helped me look for evidence of the alien in Wildcat Woods."

"It's not been that long, but it seems like a lifetime ago." He took the canister and coated himself.

"So many things have changed in one summer." I set the can on the shelf, and we walked outside under the canopy of trees.

The cicadas droned in symphony, and Hemi took my hand as we strolled the driveway. "I'm excited for what's next. Not just for my teaching job but for spending more time with you."

"I really haven't scared you off?"

"Nope."

"Good. But you should know, after everything that's happened this summer, I've been rethinking the whole investigative reporter gig. Being a regular reporter or a freelance writer and mom would suit me fine."

"Whatever makes you happy."

He couldn't quite hide the relief in his voice and eyes, and I didn't mind because it showed me how much he cared.

When we reached the road, he said, "Bobbi Sue, I know we haven't been together for long, so it's too soon to propose—"

"Because my dad would kill you."

"If my mom didn't get to me first."

I laughed and then bit my tongue. Literally.

"But—I need you to know. I'm in this relationship for the long haul. I don't know what'll happen after you graduate from college next spring, but as far as I'm concerned, we'll figure it out. Because you're my girl."

"And you're my guy." I stopped along the side of the road and faced him. Twilight painted the sky, and the trees swayed in the breeze.

He bent to kiss me. Then, he grasped my hand as we continued our stroll through Wildcat Woods.

The summer of 1988 in Wildcat Springs gave me more than I ever could've anticipated—and proved that no matter what I'd once believed, life here would never, *ever* be boring.

Don't miss out on any of my new mysteries. Stay in touch by subscribing to my e-mail newsletter, where you'll get the latest information about my new releases. As a thank you for subscribing, you'll gain access to *Deadly Homestead: A Georgia Rae Winston Mini-Mystery and Other Short Stories*.

If you enjoyed *It Happened One Plight*, I'd be very appreciative if you'd leave a brief review to help me spread the word about my novels.

ABOUT THE AUTHOR

Jenni Mansell Photography

Marissa Shrock is a survivor of many awkward blind dates and many years of teaching middle school. Both provide excellent inspiration for her fictional yarns.

Since childhood, she's loved to read a variety of genres, so her own work includes dystopian thrillers and cozy mysteries. She's the author of the Emancipation Warriors Series, the Georgia Rae Winston Mysteries, and the Bobbi Sue Baxter Mysteries. Her debut novel, *The First Principle,* was a Carol Award Finalist.

Marissa enjoys playing golf, building elaborate LEGO creations, and traveling to new places. Visit her at www.marissashrock.com.

ALSO BY MARISSA SHROCK

Georgia Rae Winston Mystery Series

Deadly Harvest

Deadly Holiday

Deadly Heritage

Deadly Harmony

Deadly Hideaway

Deadly Heartbreak

Bobbi Sue Baxter Mysteries

Close Encounters of the Murderous Kind

The Body Electrocution

The Edge of Knife

It Happened One Plight

CREDITS

Editing by A Little Red Ink

Cover Art by Sweet 'N Spicy Designs

Cimelia Press Logo by Race Point

Beta Readers: Brad and Mary Shrock

www.ingramcontent.com/pod-product-compliance
Lightning Source LLC
LaVergne TN
LVHW090605110826
845146LV00001B/270

* 9 7 9 8 9 9 2 1 3 0 5 1 5 *